Moloka'i

Lana'i

Maui

Kaho'olawe

Mauna Kea

Kailua-Kona ○   **Hawai'i**   ○ **Hilo**

Volcanoes NP

Moloka'i

Lana'i

Maui

Kaho'olawe

Mauna Kea

Kailua-Kona ○   Hawai'i   ○ Hilo

Volcanoes NP

TRAVELS WITH GANNON & WYATT

HAWAII

PATTI WHEELER & KEITH HEMSTREET

GREENLEAF
BOOK GROUP PRESS

Published by Greenleaf Book Group Press
Austin, Texas
www.gbgpress.com

Copyright ©2016 Claim Stake Productions

Distributed by Greenleaf Book Group

For ordering information or special discounts for bulk purchases, please contact Greenleaf Book Group at PO Box 91869, Austin, TX 78709, 512.891.6100.

Design and composition by Greenleaf Book Group
Cover design by Greenleaf Book Group

Publisher's Cataloging-In-Publication Data

ISBN 13: 978-1-62634-307-8

eBook ISBN: 978-1-62634-308-5

Part of the Tree Neutral® program, which offsets the number of trees consumed in the production and printing of this book by taking proactive steps, such as planting trees in direct proportion to the number of trees used: www.treeneutral.com.

Printed in the United States of America on acid-free paper

16 17 18 19 20 19 20 21 10 9 8 7 6 5 4 3 2 1

First Edition

ENGLISH/HAWAIIAN:
TRANSLATION OF COMMON PHRASES

Good morning—Aloha kakahiaka

Good afternoon—Aloha ʻauinalā

Good evening—Aloha ahiahi

Goodbye—A hui hou kākou

You're welcome—ʻAʻole pilikia

What is your name?—ʻO wai kou inoa?

Thank you—Mahalo

Thank you very much—Mahalo nui loa

Good luck—Laki maikaʻi

We are truly blessed/fortunate—Pōmaikaʻi loa kākou

Turtle—Honu

Foreigner, Caucasian—Laki maikaʻi

Land—ʻĀina

Family—ʻOhana

Child—Keiki

To adopt—Hānai

An adopted child—Keiki Hānai

Parent—Makua

Grandpa, or Grandma—Tūtū

"ALOHA," as as interepreted into an acrostic poem by Pilahi Paki

A is for **Akahai**, or *gentle and kindly*

L is for **Lōkahi**, or *unity*

O is for **'Olu'olu**, or *pleasantness*

H is for **Ha'aha'a**, or *humility*

A is for **Ahonui**, or *patience*

Ua mau ke ea o ka ʻāina i ka pono

The life of the land is perpetuated in righteousness

An ʻōlelo noʻeau, or wise saying, uttered by King Kamehameha III in 1843 and eventually became the motto for the State of Hawaiʻi.

CONTENTS

PART I

THE LAND OF FIRE AND ICE

WYATT

FEBRUARY 3, 8:22 PM
MAUNA KEA, HAWAII 19° 07' N 155° 81' W
24° FAHRENHEIT, -5° CELSIUS
ELEVATION: 13,796 FT.
WIND: 20-30 MPH

I t snows in Hawaii. Most people don't realize this, but it's true. There are a few places on these lush, tropical islands where it snows, sometimes heavily.

"We sure did pick a fine day to climb a volcano!" Gannon shouted, as heavy white flakes blew sideways in the wind.

I could hardly breathe, much less respond. Suffering the effects of high altitude, I trekked on as best I could. At an elevation of nearly fourteen thousand feet above sea level the oxygen is so thin just putting one foot in front of the other requires tremendous physical effort. The process goes like this: Inhale, take a short step, exhale, and repeat.

The driving snow kept getting stuck in my eyelashes,

making it nearly impossible to see. My hands and feet were numb. A sharp pain shot through my chest with each gasping breath. It literally felt like I was dragging a bus behind me.

An unexpected blizzard moves over the ridge

The conditions on the slopes of Mauna Kea had gone from decent to deadly in a matter of minutes. Making the situation worse, we didn't have the necessary gear to weather a blizzard. My brother and I had worn waterproof shells with fleece lining, but had forgotten to bring several other pieces of crucial equipment. Namely, goggles, thermal socks, and warmer gloves. The Big Island of Hawaii contains four of the earth's five major climate zones—from tropical to polar.

I knew this, but before we set off on our hike, I had not fully considered just how severe the weather might be near the summit.

As the FIRST LAW OF EXPLORATION states, know your destination. Well, I know my destination, studied it for well over a month before we arrived. My mom had also given us several homeschool assignments related to the geography, ecosystem, and culture of Hawaii, yet I still managed to embark on this trek ill-equipped for a polar climate. I have to admit, it was a total amateur move.

Not to make excuses, but Hawaii, in all of its tropical beauty, can lull you into a state similar to a mild hypnosis, where you just go with the flow, assuming that everything will be all right. Hawaiians have a real "no worries" attitude and it's hard not to adopt it when you spend time here. Don't get me wrong, I do appreciate it, but for an explorer that kind of attitude can spell disaster.

"I can't feel my hands," I slurred, my face numbed by the cold. "These thin gloves we brought aren't doing any good!"

"Sorry, I can't hear you!" Gannon yelled. "I think my ears just froze off!"

As my feet sunk into the fresh snow, it was hard to believe that we had started the day in flip flops and shorts, swimming in the turquoise bay in the town of Kailua-Kona. Even now, a mere thirty miles from where we stood, people were splashing around in the Pacific Ocean, enjoying the warmth on one of Hawaii's spectacular beaches.

It was at the Mauna Kea Visitor Center (9,200 feet) that Gannon and I decided to hike to the summit. The air was cool at the visitor center, 48°F, and the sky was blue. Air temperature drops approximately 3.5 degrees every thousand feet of elevation, so by my calculation, it was about 31°F atop Mauna Kea's 13,976-foot summit. Cold, for sure, but nothing to be overly concerned about.

Or so we thought.

Mauna Kea happens to be one of the best locations in the world to view the stars. Most nights are clear and there is almost no light pollution. The girl working at the visitor center was a native Hawaiian from the island of Kauai. Her name was Margaret. At our request, she put in a call to the renowned astronomer Dr. Peter Ward, who is stationed at the University of Hawaii observatory near the summit. On the flight from Los Angeles, we had read about the university's telescope, one of the most powerful in the world, so naturally we were ecstatic when Dr. Ward told Margaret he'd be happy to give us a tour. He did warn us of some approaching weather and dropping temps, but we thought nothing of it. When our family is not traveling, we live at eight thousand feet in the Rocky Mountains where it is cold and snowy all winter long. We have grown up skiing and snowshoeing, and have taken a number of winter expeditions into the backcountry. Gannon and I are comfortable in the mountains. It's our backyard. Hawaii couldn't throw anything at us that we hadn't seen before, could it?

Well, here's something to remember: At high altitude anything can happen.

"I can't go any further!" Gannon shouted into the blinding storm. "Hypothermia is setting in! I can feel it! We have to take shelter!"

Gannon was right. I was chilled to the bone. If we became hypothermic, our lives would be in real danger.

A small herd of mouflon, which look like big horned sheep, materialized in the white flakes then disappeared just as quickly. To our left I could make out Lake Waiau, a small, heart-shaped body of green water with a thin crust of ice along the shore. The summit of Mauna Kea has a smooth moonlike surface, so it didn't seem likely that we'd find a cave, but a few feet of snow had accumulated on a nearby north-facing slope. It was the perfect place to make a shelter.

"Only option is to dig a snow cave!" I called out.

"Whatever!" Gannon snapped. "Let's just be quick about it!"

Gannon and I knelt in the snow and began to dig. Scooping away piles at a time, a small cave began to form. The cold went right through my thin gloves. My hands ached. I shook them to relieve the pain. As soon as the cave was big enough for Gannon and I to huddle next to each other, we wedged ourselves inside. Can't say it was any warmer in the cave, but it did protect us from the wind.

Snow cave on Mauna Kea

"I c-c-can read the headline now," Gannon said, his jaw quivering. "Two b-b-boneheaded explorers freeze to death on Hawaii's s-s-sacred mountain."

"We'll be fine as long as the storm b-b-blows through!" I shouted.

"And what if it d-d-doesn't? We could be stuck here! We don't have enough gear to survive a night of s-s-sub-f-f-freezing temperatures."

"P-P-Panicking isn't going to help our situation, G-G-Gannon."

"Oh, jeez, you know what I bet's going on here?" Gannon blurted. "We've offended P-P- Poli'ahu!"

"Who?"

"Poli'ahu, the Goddess of M-M-Mauna Kea. Don't you know anything about Hawaiian c-c-culture? We never asked her permission to climb to the summit."

"This storm isn't the work of a Goddess, Gannon! It was created by an atmospheric c-c-condition in which moisture and warm air from the Pacific Ocean collides with c-c-colder air at high altitude and . . . "

"Please, b-b-bro! Poli'ahu isn't in the m-m-mood to listen to your nerdy scientific explanation, and neither am I!"

Gannon hopped up and ran back into the storm. At the edge of the lake, he knelt down and opened his arms to the sky.

"Oh, Poli'ahu, Goddess of Mauna Kea!" Gannon hollered. "We have come to honor you! Please grant us safe passage to the summit! I promise, if we make it off this volcano alive, we will spread word of Hawaii's rich culture and beautiful environment to young people around the world!"

When Gannon crawled back into the snow cave, I rolled my eyes.

"Nice, Gannon," I said. "I bet it will stop snowing any minute now."

Oddly enough, it did.

What had quickly become a terrible storm had just as quickly diminished to a light flurry. The wind died down and patches of blue sky appeared. Gannon stared at me, a smirk on his face. I knew he was waiting for some kind of acknowledgement, so I ignored him.

"You're welcome," he finally said.

"Seriously, you're going to try to take credit?" I asked, almost laughing.

"If you respect indigenous cultures and their beliefs, your travels will be rewarded. You know who said that?"

"Who?"

"I did."

"Sorry, but the fact that this storm suddenly let up has *nothing* to do with all the babbling you just did."

"Hey, everything I said was true. If the Youth Exploration Society publishes our field notes, kids all over the world will be able to read about these incredible islands. So, let's make sure our notes are good enough for publication. After all, I have to keep my word to Poli'ahu. Now let's get to the summit before we're walloped by another storm."

Continuing our strenuous hike, we moved along the ridge of the summit cone, one slow step at a time. Above us the sky cleared. Below us was the Pacific, vast and blue and sparkling under the late afternoon sun. Over our shoulder was Mauna Kea's snowcapped sister, Mauna Loa, which rises to 13,678 feet and is still "active."

My brother was a good ten feet ahead of me when he took his place atop the mountain's highest point. Interesting fact: If you measure Mauna Kea from the bottom of the ocean it is 32,696 feet high, making it the tallest mountain in the world, even taller than Mt. Everest, which stands at 29,035 feet!

When I met Gannon at the summit, he held up his hand for a high-five. My thin fleece gloves were doing little to protect my hands, which were swollen and stinging from the extreme altitude and cold. Giving Gannon five sent a pain through my hand so severe it almost brought tears to my eyes. But the pain quickly faded. The excitement was just too great.

"We did it, bro!" Gannon said, gasping for breath. "We summited Mauna Kea! Wow, this is pretty amazing!"

Knowing that these moments never last, I took some time to appreciate where I stood—atop the highest point in Hawaii, on the most geographically remote landmass on earth. For me, to be in this most unexpected of climates—the polar zone of Hawaii—was reason enough to embark on this journey.

The lowest temperature ever recorded on Mauna Kea was 12°F back in 1978, and we weren't too far from that record. My thermometer read 24°F. On the far horizon, orange sky was mixed with streaks of pink and purple. Higher up the sky was an indigo shade of blue. It would be dark soon.

"We better get to the observatory," I said. "Dr. Ward is probably wondering what happened to us."

"Hold on," Gannon said and knelt in the snow. "I need to thank Poli'ahu. You know, for not freezing us solid in that blizzard and all."

Gannon started to gather snow with his hands, groaning in pain as he packed up a set of snowballs.

"What are you doing?" I asked.

"You'll see," he said.

On top of a rock at the summit of Mauna Kea, Gannon built a small snowman. From his pocket he removed the frond of a palm tree and used it to make a small scarf that he wrapped around the snowman's neck.

"There," he said, stepping back to admire his work. "The palm scarf makes this snowman uniquely Hawaiian, don't you think?"

"It's a nice touch."

"Poli'ahu," Gannon said, looking to the sky. "This snowman is for you. His name is . . . Morty 'Little Kahuna' Mauna Kea."

I shook my head.

"Why Morty?" I asked.

"He just looks like a Morty, doesn't he?"

After staring at him for a minute, I have to admit, he did kind of look like a Morty.

The darkness was settling fast and we didn't have our headlamps with us, so we hiked down from the summit with shaky legs to the University of Hawaii's observatory. It's a shame that I am too tired to write more, as I'm just getting to the best part of today's experience, the spectacular galaxy gazing, and would love to document it in detail. But Dr. Ward gave me a map of our solar system and a book on the history of astronomy, so I'm leaving with lots of valuable information. In brief, it was an experience so fascinating it has made me consider a future in astronomy. After all, I am an aspiring scientist, as well as an explorer, and space *is* the final frontier. Given the technological advances in space travel predicted in our lifetime, it's not unrealistic to think that I might one day have the chance to travel to a distant planet.

Right now, though, I can hardly keep my eyes open. As I write my final words of the day, we're still awaiting a call that the snowplows have finished clearing the roads. Once they give the "all clear," we're hitching a ride down the mountain in Dr. Ward's four-wheel drive.

More tomorrow, but for now, from high above the Pacific Ocean, I am fading fast and must say, "Goodnight!"

Morty 'Little Kahuna' Mauna Kea

GANNON

Okay, let's see. Where should I begin my Hawaii journal? Hmmm.

Well, since I can't seem to make a decision, I should probably just put pen to paper and start writing whatever comes to mind, which is what I'm doing now, I guess. Right, so . . . doodling . . . chewing on pen cap . . . ah-ha, I got it!

A great place to start would be to transcribe the letter we got from Alana, which basically sums up our mission while in Hawaii. I have her letter right here, folded in my journal.

Alana is a member of the Youth Exploration Society (Y.E.S.) and will guide us on an expedition beginning tomorrow. About a month ago, we wrote to the Y.E.S. office in Kailua-Kona requesting a guide and information on the cultural and environmental issues facing the Hawaiian Islands. A couple weeks later, we received the following letter:

```
Dear Gannon & Wyatt,

My name is Alana Aukai, and I am a certified
Hawaiian guide with the Youth Exploration
Society. It will be my pleasure to show
you the many cultural and environmental
treasures on the Big Island. I would suggest
a visit to Volcanoes National Park, a trek
to an active lava flow, a hike through a
```

tropical rainforest, and maybe a snorkeling excursion that will give you the chance to view dolphins, sea turtles, and sharks. If it suits you, I would be happy to schedule a day of surfing and arrange a hula lesson.

I should also mention a recent development that may be of interest to you. There is a group of scientists currently searching for the bones of King Kamehameha the Great. At the time of the King's death in 1819, the location of his burial site was kept secret in order to protect his spiritual "mana," or power. Today, many Hawaiians are worried that if found, the King's remains will be removed from the island. It is very important to the people of the islands that our Royal heritage be respected and preserved. As I said, a search is underway, and we will be sure to stay on top of the progress as we tour the island.

I look very forward to your visit and promise you a wonderful adventure.

Mahalo,
Alana

Um, how about yes to all of the above! Except maybe the whole snorkeling with sharks thing. I'm not too keen on that, but it did just give me an idea for a joke.

—*What does a shark call a snorkeler?*

—*His chum.*

Ha, get it? I know, I know, pretty lame joke. And I know sharks don't actually like to eat humans (I guess we don't taste very good), but they've still been known to take a bite out of us on occasion, so I'd rather not take my chances. As for the rest of Alana's itinerary, I'm totally up for it.

Okay, some quick math . . . let's see, if we arrived last night that would mean we've been here a total of twenty-four hours, give or take, so I think I'll go ahead and put down on paper my first impression of Hawaii, which is that it's one of the most adventure-seeking, good-vibe-feeling, soul-healing places on the face of the planet. I mean, really, there's so much to it—mountains, snow, volcanoes, rainforests, deserts, waterfalls, rivers, ranchlands, rainbows, beaches, reefs, a fascinating culture, cool people, exotic birds, colorful fish, fragrant flowers—in a word, Hawaii has *everything*!

As much as I would have enjoyed soaking up some rays on the beach with my parents today, Wyatt and I were itching to begin our explorations. And since we're not meeting Alana until tomorrow we set off alone, catching a ride to the visitor center high on the slopes of Hawaii's sacred mountain, where we wound up biting off a little more adventure than we could chew. I'd go into detail, but just before Wyatt slumped over in his chair and started snoring like a mule, he told me he wrote all about our climb in his journal, so I won't get into all that again, other than to say that between the trek to the top of the Mauna Kea (which means "White Mountain" in Hawaiian), battling frostbite and hypothermia, my plea to Poli'ahu to please, please, please spare us our lives, and having the chance to build a snowman (in Hawaii of all places!), I didn't think it was possible to pack another ounce of awesomeness into this delirious frenzy of a day.

Well, I was wrong, because when we got the chance to take a peek through one of the most powerful telescopes ever built, *THE STARS NEARLY BLEW MY MIND!*

For real, from here on out I will encourage any kid who has access to a telescope to spend some serious time gazing at the heavens. The experience has given me a new perspective on what a small space we occupy in this infinitely vast universe of ours.

Falling ice is a hazard outside the observatories

Being inside the observatory is kind of like being inside a huge dome. There's a set of stairs in the center of the observatory, which lead up to a big metal contraption that looks sort of like a crane. This crane-looking thing is what holds the telescope in position. The white dome roof is retractable, so you can open it to view the stars or close it off when the weather is bad.

Dr. Peter Ward is a very smart, gray-haired, bifocal-wearing gentleman who is highly respected in the astronomy world for making all kinds of new discoveries related to stars and planets and galaxies and stuff like that. He runs the University of Hawaii's observatory and greeted us with open arms when we arrived. Of course, my geeky, science-loving brother was all giddy to pick his brain, but I wanted to skip the scientific jibber-jabber and get right to the good part—viewing the stars at close range!

"So, Dr. Ward, what am I looking at here?" I asked, as I peered into the telescope.

"What you're looking at is the planet Mars," Dr. Ward said. "I was observing the planet's topography when you arrived. Mars isn't always visible because of its orbit around the sun, so this is a real treat."

"Wow, Mars, huh? It kind of looks like a big red moon."

"Take a look at this image," Dr. Ward said, pointing to a large computer screen. "It is from an unmanned Rover mission that actually touched down on Mars. What you see here is the surface of the planet."

On the screen was a photo of a treeless, shrubless, mountainous landscape with thousands of small rocks scattered about in red dirt. In some ways it looked like the Sahara Desert in North Africa.

Wyatt had another take.

"Sort of looks like Mauna Kea when there's no snow," he said.

"Indeed," Dr. Ward said, "Mars is barren and mountainous, much like the high altitudes of Mauna Kea."

I walked back and looked into the telescope again.

"Oh, my gosh, Wyatt!"

"What is it?"

"A Martian!"

Wyatt scoffed.

"Very funny, Gannon."

Okay, fine. I was joking, but the joke actually got me thinking. Dr. Ward told us there are hundreds of billions of stars in our galaxy and at least another hundred billion galaxies beyond our own, give or take. So, really, who can say for sure whether or not there's some other form of intelligent life out there?

"So, uh, Dr. Ward," I said, peering again through the telescope. "Have you ever seen an alien spaceship zipping through the sky?"

"Not yet," Dr. Ward said with a chuckle.

Wyatt stepped up and shoved me out of the way.

"Let me have a turn," he said through clenched teeth. "And stop asking such ridiculous questions."

"Jeez, lighten up," I said. "Besides, it's not a ridiculous question."

"I said *zip it*."

As he gazed at Mars, he asked all kinds of scientific questions I didn't understand. After a while, Dr. Ward pushed a few buttons and the telescope shifted several feet.

"Have a look now," he said.

What we saw through the telescope looked a lot like a canyon in the sky made up of narrow, jagged dark spaces outlined by the bright white light of a bazillion stars!

"Wow, what's that?" I asked.

"It's the galaxy that contains the sun and our own solar system," Wyatt said, "otherwise known as the Milky Way."

"Very good, Wyatt," Dr. Ward said.

"Whoa, I had no idea the Milky Way looked like that!"

The Milky Way

Dr. Ward then pointed out a number of stars and constellations, including the North Star and the Big Dipper.

"The North Star never moves," Dr. Ward explained. "It remains constant in the sky, while all the other stars rotate around it counterclockwise. That is why the North Star was so important to the Polynesians and others who traveled by sea. They used it for navigation."

"That's so cool," I said.

For some reason, my eyes were drawn to a little flickering star way, way off in the far reaches.

"Dr. Ward, what's the name of this star?" I asked, and pointed to it. "The one in the upper right corner that's flickering red, white, and yellow?"

Dr. Ward looked into the telescope and made a note of the star's location.

"I'll have to look it up on the chart," he said, and scanned a massive map of the stars that was sprawled out across a table.

"Funny you should point that one out, Gannon," he said. "That's a newer star, and it happens to be unnamed. Would you boys like to do the honor?"

"Absolutely!" Wyatt said.

"For sure!" I said.

"Then why don't you come up with a name together?" Dr. Ward said.

"I appreciate the suggestion, Doctor," Wyatt said. "But it's highly unlikely that my brother and I would ever agree on a name."

"That's true," I said. "Let's rock, paper, scissors. Best out of five. Whoever wins gets to name the star."

"You're on. Ready? Rock, paper, scissors, shoot!"

Oh, man. I swept my brother like a broom sweeps dirt. Took him 3-0. Wyatt, who can't stand losing, walked away in a huff.

"Do you have a name in mind, Gannon?" Dr. Ward asked.

"Let's see. Given that this star was discovered from atop Mauna Kea, I think it's fitting that the name should be Hawaiian."

I looked through the telescope again.

"You know, to me the sky kind of looks like a dark ocean and the stars look like these little, twinkly fish, which gives me an idea. Dr. Ward, do you know the state fish of Hawaii?"

"I do, in fact. It's the *humuhumunukunukuāpuaʻa*."

"Excuse me?" I said.

The doctor laughed.

"It's a mouthful, I know. I'll repeat it very slowly. Humu-humu-nuku-nuku-ā-puaʻa."

"Well, all righty then," I said, turning to Wyatt with a grin. "I hereby name this newly discovered star whatever it is that Dr. Ward just said, in honor of Hawaii's state fish."

"I will make official record of it in the International Astronomical Union's database tomorrow," Dr. Ward said, "giving you full credit of course."

"Thank you, Doctor," I said with a bow.

Oh, man, for me to get credit for anything scientific really boils Wyatt's blood. I mean, science is his field of expertise, not mine. On the surface, he seemed to keep his cool about it, but underneath that thin skin of his, I could tell he was fuming.

Dr. Ward is speaking to students at the Hawaiian Preparatory Academy in Waimea early tomorrow morning. He's driving there tonight and is going to drop us off in Kailua-Kona where we'll reconnect with our parents. Tomorrow mid-morning sometime we'll meet up with Alana and set off on our mission to learn all about the history, culture, and environment of the Hawaiian Islands.

As I said already, day one has been totally epic, but truth is, our adventure has only just begun! When I think of the week ahead, I get so wound up I can hardly control myself.

Okay, just got word that the roads have been cleared, so

it's about time to head back down to sea level where the oxygen is more plentiful and the air is nice and warm.

So, for now, I guess this is goodbye . . . or as the native Hawaiians say, *A hui hou kākou.*

WYATT

FEBRUARY 4, 10:04 AM
KAILUA-KONA, HAWAII 19° 07' N 155° 81' W
78° FAHRENHEIT, 26° CELSIUS
ELEVATION: SEA LEVEL

The Big Island of Hawaii is a place of incredible diversity. Last night Gannon and I were knee-deep in snow, worried we might freeze to death. This morning I'm in shorts on the balmy Kona coast, perspiring as a warm sea breeze blows over the deck of the beachside café where we're having breakfast.

"Everyone listen," my dad said, and cupped his hand behind his ear. "You hear that?"

Fronds of the high coconut palms rustled in the wind. Rolling waves moved up and over the lava rocks just off the deck. From the nearby trees came the distinct calls of various birds.

My dad continued, "That's the soothing sounds of nature, boys. In my opinion, there's nothing better."

Not far offshore, a dozen or more people were getting their morning exercise, swimming from one side of the bay to the other.

"What a great way to start your day," my mom said, pointing to the swimmers.

"Goes without saying," my dad commented, "But I'm a big fan of these islands."

"Me too," Gannon said. "Just glad we survived the blizzard yesterday."

"Yeah, about that," my mom said. "I noticed your cheeks are wind burned. Was it really that cold on Mauna Kea?"

"You know, mom, I'm not one to repeat myself . . ."

"Yes you are," I said, quickly interjecting to correct my brother's false statement.

"Okay, fine. Maybe I am. Point is, Mom, since you're grading our journals before we submit them to the Youth Exploration Society, I'd rather not spoil the surprise. Wyatt and I spent a lot of time writing last night. I promise, you can read all about it soon."

"It sounds like your journals are off to a great start," she said. "Keep it up because they are going to be a large part of your writing grade this semester. Your environmental science and history grades, too."

"Don't worry," I said. "I expect top grades, as usual. As for Gannon and his run-on sentences and excessive use of hyperbole, well . . ."

"Hold on just a sec!" Gannon interrupted. "First of all, when I write I want to capture the true emotion of the experience. If I use a run-on sentence here and there, so be it. Second, what the heck is hyperbole?"

"Just about everything you write and say is hyperbole."

"*Hele pēlā*, Wyatt," Gannon said, brushing me off with a wave of his hand.

"What does that mean?" I asked.

"Why don't you look it up?"

"All right you two," my Dad said. "Knock it off."

Here I must go on record and say just how much I dislike it when my brother insults me in a language that I don't understand. That said, I must give him props. He's getting pretty good at it.

We're meeting our guide Alana shortly at the farmer's market in town. Afterwards, my mom flies to Oahu where she will work as the lead flight attendant on the Honolulu-Tokyo route for World Airlines. When she returns midweek, she's volunteering at the Hawaiian Cultural Center in Honolulu where they are hosting a workshop that teaches young people the native language. At breakfast, my mom was reading a book written by a Hawaiian linguist and passed on some interesting facts.

"Back in the 1920s and 30s the islands were colonized by people from Europe, Japan, and the United States," my mom explained. "At the time, they felt the Hawaiian language was useless and banned it from schools. For decades, it wasn't taught and people were discouraged from using it."

"Oh, come on," Gannon said, smacking the table. "How could anyone think that a native language is useless? That's ridiculous!"

"Well, they were wrong, of course. The Hawaiian language is beautiful and rich with meaning, but today only a small number of Hawaiians speak it fluently. The good people at the Cultural Center want to change that, and since I love languages myself, I volunteered to help."

"Mom," Gannon said, "I almost wish I was coming with you, but there's no way I can pass up exploring this island with Alana. And she said there's a group of scientists searching for the bones of King Kamehameha the Great, which is crazy to even think about!"

"Don't worry. You can join me next week in Oahu. There will still be some time to take part in the workshop before we fly home."

"Oh, and while we're there, I also want to visit the Pearl Harbor War Memorial."

"It's an absolute must. Besides, it will be part of the history exam I'm giving you both when we get home."

Since we travel so much, my mom homeschools Gannon and me, which is great, most of the time. It's only a problem when she piles on the work, like she's doing now.

This afternoon my dad is catching a ride to the northern part of the island, where he will be staying in a simple hut about two thousand feet above sea level. There is no phone service or television on the property. In fact, there is no electricity, period, only a few solar lamps and candles. The water used for showers and drinking is recaptured rain. For a bathroom, there is a compost outhouse. It's what my dad calls an "off the grid" retreat. Here's a photo the owner sent him.

Dad's accommodations

Living without modern conveniences doesn't really faze my dad. It's quite the opposite, actually. He loves it. From his hut he said he'll be able to look out over the island of Maui, enjoy spectacular sunsets and see dozens of shooting stars each night. Somewhere on the hillside, he'll set up his easel and canvases and work on a series of Hawaiian landscapes that he's been commissioned to paint for an art collector in San Francisco. Painting and sculpture are my dad's passion and he always reminds us how wonderful it is that he gets to do it for a living.

I better sign off here. It's time to go meet Alana. Lots of ground to cover this week. "Volcanic" ground, to be more precise!

GANNON

Oh, man, this morning started off as one of those days where I wake up with so much energy pulsing though my body it almost catapults me out of bed, and this despite having incredibly sore legs from yesterday's climb. While I was getting dressed and brushing my teeth, I had this huge smile on my face and was so amped to go outside and explore I could hardly focus.

This sort of thing happens most often when I'm in a place I've never been before. It's the *newness* of it all, I think, and newness seems to have some kind of transformative power. Like it's actually good for your brain. Come to think of it, Wyatt told me something about it once, and he's pretty smart when it comes to that kind of stuff. What he said, as best I can remember, was that new experiences create pathways between different parts of your brain, or something like that. What I think that means is that new experiences excite, open, and expand our minds. They give us a heightened sense of awareness and allow us to see and think differently. Basically, new experiences help make us smarter.

Okay, enough with the neuroscience mumbo jumbo. That's Wyatt's department. My areas of interest are travel (of course), people, culture, language, nature, filmmaking, writing, etc. So, like any explorer worth a darn, I've got to document today's experience.

So here goes . . .

Old town Kailua-Kona is a stretch of low-rise cottages, hotels, restaurants, and storefronts with some serious royal history. At the far end of the bay, near the pier, is the former dwelling place of King Kamehameha the Great, the powerful and mighty warrior responsible for bringing all of the Hawaiian Islands together under one ruler. At the edge of the water is a replica village with thatched roof huts that supposedly resembles what was here during the reign of the King.

Stopping to look around, I found it hard to imagine King Kamehameha ruling the Hawaiian Islands from this place. I mean, no offense to anyone or anything, it's just that the historic significance of the place was kind of diminished by the huge concrete hotel, swimming pool, and shopping mall that now surround it.

Replica hut in Kailua-Kona

Flip-flopping our way toward the market, skateboarders and bikers mingled with slow moving cars. The sidewalks were sprinkled with all these little white and yellow flowers. My mom said they were called plumeria and made us stop and notice the flower's sweet fragrance in the breeze. The bay was as clear as a swimming pool with schools of bright yellow fish swimming along the seawall. Further out, people paddled outrigger canoes in deep blue water that sparkled in the sun. Anchored offshore, a few yachts and sailboats rocked casually in the waves.

About midway down the boardwalk we came to a massive magnolia tree, its canopy of leaves stretching up and over the street and littering everything underneath with squishy red seeds. The tree actually stands on the grounds of the Hulihe'e Palace, a modest royal home built in the late 1800s. Just across the street from the palace is a beautiful old church with a high white steeple.

Downtown Kailua-Kona

A minute or so from the palace, we came to the local market. I guess Alana had seen photos of Wyatt and me in the Youth Exploration Society archives, because as soon as she saw us cross the street she came running. She had four flower leis draped over her arm and she flipped us that cool Hawaiian "hang loose" sign, the one where you curl your middle fingers into your palm, extend your thumb and pinky finger and wiggle your hand back and forth.

"Aloha!" Alana said.

"Aloha," all four of us responded at once.

"Welcome to Hawaii," she said, placing flower leis over our heads one by one.

"Thank you, Alana," Wyatt said. "It's a pleasure to be here."

"And a pleasure to meet you," I added.

"The pleasure is all mine," she said. "After I wrote you, I found your field notes in the Youth Exploration Society library and read all about your adventures. Very impressive."

"That's kind of you to say," Wyatt replied, blushing slightly.

"Alana," my dad said, "I'd love to know the story behind the gesture you just made with your hand."

He demonstrated the wave.

"That's the shaka sign," Alana said. "It was made popular decades ago by Hawaiian surfers."

"Is it just a Hawaiian greeting, like waving *hello*?" he asked.

"Yes, it is, but more importantly shaka is another way to express the Aloha Spirit."

"What's the Aloha Spirit?" I asked.

"When you pass someone on the street and offer the shaka sign or say 'Aloha' it is a gesture of friendship, compassion and acceptance of all people and cultures. It is also the sharing of life's great energy and the recognition that we are always in the presence of God. Each and every day, we Hawaiians strive to embody the Aloha Spirit."

"That's beautiful," my mom said, almost tearing up.

"It really is," my dad added.

In all my cultural investigations, the "Aloha Spirit" is honestly one of the greatest things I've ever come across. I mean, seriously, just imagine what a peaceful world it would be if everyone embraced the "Aloha Spirit."

Alana has dark hair, which she had pulled back into a long ponytail, bronze, sun-kissed skin, and beautiful hazel eyes that glow like a light was shining through them. She wore a white top and red and white flowered sarong, which is basically a sheet of material that you wrap around your waist like a skirt. On her feet was a pair of flip flops.

"You know, Alana," Wyatt mumbled, still a little taken aback by her beauty, "maybe during our expedition you can help with my study of the Hawaiian flora, fauna, and native bird species."

I leaned in close to Wyatt's ear.

"Little heavy on the nerdiness, bro," I whispered.

"What are you talking about?" he asked, quietly.

Sometimes Wyatt is so clueless.

"You're being a total haole," I said. "That's what I'm talking about."

"What's a haole?" Wyatt asked, a hint of frustration in his tone.

On the flight over, I'd studied a handful of Hawaiian words and phrases. Haole (pronounced *how-lee*) basically means "foreigner" or "white person," but it's also used by Hawaiians to describe tourists when they behave, oh, I don't know . . . like tourists.

"Well, Gannon," Alana said to me with a smile, "By definition, you are a haole, too."

"Okay, true. But, trust me, I'm less of one than my brother is. You'll see."

Wyatt's ears got all red and he had that look on his face like he'd just caught a whiff of something stinky. I've seen that face a thousand times. It's his "mad face."

He moved close and jabbed me in the ribs with his elbow.

"Jeez," I said, reacting to the blow. "That was totally uncalled for."

"You better tell me what that word means right now," Wyatt whispered through clinched teeth.

"Look it up in your Hawaiian phrase book?"

"I didn't bring one."

"Ahhh, too bad."

Alana was chuckling.

"Sorry to break this up," she said, "but what do you say we begin our journey? We have lots to do and see. After we explore the Pololū Valley today, you will get to meet my mother. She'll update us on the search for the bones of King Kamehameha the Great."

"Have they found anything?" Wyatt asked.

"Not yet, but apparently one of the scientists believes he is close."

"Okay, I'm with Alana," I said, clapping my hands together. "Let's get going. Adventure awaits!"

Little early to say for sure, but I'm thinking Alana might turn out to be our best guide ever, and that's high praise because we've had some top-notch guides in our day. Here's the thing about Alana, not only is she sweet and easy to talk to and super knowledgeable about all things Hawaiian, she also has this totally awesome convertible jeep! I honestly can't imagine a better vehicle for a tour of the Big Island!

"Remember," my mom said, wagging her finger at us. "Be safe, learn a lot, and have a wonderful time."

Careful not to smash our leis, we hugged our parents, gave the shaka sign, and jumped into Alana's jeep. We took off from Kailua-Kona with the top down, driving north with the sun on our faces and the wind blowing through our hair. Not far from town, we started up the two-lane road that turns inland and rises along the coast. The air cooled slightly and the jeep gripped the relatively smooth blacktop that carved its way through grassy slopes and the charred remains of old lava fields. The ocean was to our left, intensely blue and spotted with white caps. Rising out of the ocean several miles off shore was a gently sloping green mountain. Alana told us this was the island of Kahoolawe, the smallest of Hawaii's eight main volcanic islands. From where we were on the Big Island, the remaining six—Maui, Lanai, Molokai, Oahu, Kauai, and

Niihau—were somewhere to our northwest, out of sight. I took out my video camera and shot some footage as we drove past sprawling ranches where cattle and horses grazed in green, windswept pastures. Ever-present to our right was the massive Mauna Kea, its summit white with snow.

It's interesting, when I visit a place like this, a place that has such a unique and beautiful landscape, I can't help but feel an immediate connection to it. I think it has to do with how I react to nature. Safe to say, I get somewhat mesmerized by it and Hawaii is easily one of the earth's most spectacular displays. It's rugged and pristine, tropical and alpine, ancient and brand new. It is no wonder Hawaiians believe their land is sacred. There's definitely something spiritual about this place. I can feel it.

Old lava flow outside Kailua-Kona

WYATT

Explorers understand that tragedy can strike in an instant. Understanding this, however, does nothing to prepare you for it. By definition, tragedy is not predictable. Tragedy sneaks up on you, walloping you when you least expect it.

Today we were reminded of that.

Kohala Mountain Road begins just outside the ranch town of Waimea, rising and falling like a roller coaster over the mountains. The road passes through forests and emerald grasslands. The Pacific Ocean and island of Maui loom large to the north, as the road winds its way down to the small town of Hawi. Without question, it is one of the most scenic stretches of road I have ever seen.

Just past Hawi we stopped at a general store for snacks and supplies, snapped a photo of the towering King Kamehameha statue, and left the jeep at the Pololū Valley lookout. That's where we picked up the Awini Trail, a series of switchbacks that descend through dense jungle all the way to the valley floor.

King Kamehameha statue, Kapaau

Steep rocky cliffs enclose the valley on both sides. A black sand beach runs for a half-mile or so between the two high walls of igneous rock. The flat valley floor is lush with palm trees and Australian pines. Alana pointed out a number of bird species native to Hawaii, like the ʻamakihi and the very rare ʻakiapolaʻau. The birds whistled and sang as they darted from one tree limb to the next.

As we marveled at these brightly colored birds, Alana gave us some surprising news.

"Did you know that Hawaii is known as the bird extinction capital of the world?"

"I didn't know that," Gannon said.

"About seventy percent of all native birds are now extinct."

"Seventy percent?" I said, in disbelief. "Why is that?"

"It's caused by invasive species and diseases that were introduced by people who came from distant lands."

"What kind of species and diseases?" Gannon asked.

"Feral cats, rats, and mongooses all kill birds. Avian malaria and pox are also big problems. Making matters worse, most of the island's forests have been cut down so the land can be used for cattle grazing. Ranching is an important part of the economy, but losing so much forest has harmed the birds and intensified a drought that's lasted several decades."

I turned to Gannon to explain.

"Studies show that forests actually create rain by attracting water vapor from nearby sources."

"What, you think I don't know that?" Gannon snapped, even though I knew he didn't.

"The good news is there are several reforestation projects in the works, which should help restore the bird populations and save the remaining species," Alana said. "You know, these islands bubbled up from volcanic vents below the ocean. Back then they were just mounds of dried lava rocks, but over time birds arrived from far away. They dropped seeds they had eaten and from those seeds forests eventually grew. It's thanks to birds that Hawaii is such a paradise, so it's only right that we do all we can to save them."

It's always troubling to learn of another environmental disaster happening on our planet. Gannon and I find them everywhere we go. Yet, at the same time it is uplifting to know that wherever there is a problem, there are also good people working together to do something about it.

Winding our way down the switchback trail, I was in awe of the environment and tropical scenery. Then, as usual, Gannon had to bring some drama to the expedition.

"Whoa!" he shouted. "Everyone stop right where you are!"

"What's the matter?" Alana asked.

"Am I the only one who sees this?" he asked, pointing at a bright yellow sign that read:

ENTERING TSUNAMI EVACUATION AREA!

"I don't know that we should go any further," Gannon said. "I mean, this place is great and all, but I don't want to risk being swept away by a tidal wave."

"We will be cautious," Alana said, with a reassuring smile. "If there is a tsunami, the alarm will sound."

Near the sign, a set of horns sat atop a high pole. The horns blast if a tidal wave is approaching.

"That's all well and good, but since the alarm won't actually stop a tsunami, what are we supposed to do if it goes off?"

"Very simple," Alana said. "Run for higher ground."

"Run for higher ground," Gannon repeated, wiggling his pointer finger. "Okay, got it. You hear that, Wyatt?"

"I did."

Gannon then turned and scanned the horizon for any unusual rise in sea level. I'll be honest, I did the same.

Tsunami warning sign

As we came closer to the valley floor, I couldn't help but imagine the three of us trying to outrun a massive wall of water as it crashed ashore. I tried to block the images and enjoy the moment, but that proved a challenge. The thought of being swallowed by a tidal wave is simply too unnerving to dismiss.

Eventually we made our way into the valley, and walked onto the grainy, black sand beach. Everywhere we went, Gannon kept pointing out the quickest path to higher ground.

"Hey, guys," he'd say. "See that little path up the hillside? Let's run for that if the alarm sounds."

"Okay, Gannon," Alana would say, kindly. "Thank you for pointing that out."

Moving inland, we cleared the shade of the tall pine trees. A few wispy clouds floated overhead. The sun warmed my face and arms. Climbing up and over a small dirt mound, a dark blue lake spread out before us. Sheltered from the wind, the lake was glassy and held an image of the surrounding green mountains on its surface. The water was cool to the touch and since we'd all worked up a good sweat, Gannon and I decided to take a quick swim. Alana, who said she never goes anywhere without wearing a bathing suit under her clothes, joined us.

The lake was clear and comfortable as we swam away from shore. Prominent jade mountains surrounded the lake on three sides. Cliffs, hundreds of thousands of years old, if not older, stood majestically against the sea.

It was just another day in paradise.

But things were about to take a turn for the worse.

After our leisurely swim we collapsed in the sand, absorbing the sun's Vitamin D as it dried our skin. A short time later, we hiked back to the beach and up a narrow trail on the opposite cliff to take in the expansive view. Traversing the cliff's edge, the waves crashed into the rocks below us, creating a booming sound as loud as thunder.

"That's some treacherous surf down there," Gannon said.

"It's not safe to swim here," Alana told us. "It's typically too rough, and there is no lifeguard on duty at this beach."

Pololū Valley cliffs

I stopped along the trail to watch the pattern of waves moving toward the island, rolling systematically, rising higher as they made their way into the shallows. Then came the explosion against rocks, the spray bursting into the air, and the white fizz of the ocean swirling as the water retreated.

Rolling over a high swell, something unusual caught my eye and then disappeared. Holding my stare for another few seconds, I saw it again. It almost looked like a person bobbing in the waves. But it couldn't be, I thought. No one in their right mind would be swimming out there.

I placed my hand atop my eyes to shield the sun's glare.

Sure enough, it *was* a person!

A *man*! And he was in trouble!

"There's someone out there in the waves!" I said, pointing.

"I see him!" Gannon shouted. "We have to do something!"

Gannon was right. Without help this man would drown. But *who* was going to save him? Alana had just told us there were no lifeguards at this beach and we weren't trained in ocean rescue. My heart began to beat faster as I thought through our options.

Quickly, I faced the facts. We were his only hope.

From where we stood on the cliff, there was a clear path to jump into the ocean. Problem was, if we did jump in and try to help this man we could drown ourselves.

What do you do in this situation?

Every cell in my body was screaming to help this man. He kept getting pulled underneath. Each time he went under I knew his chances of coming back up were reduced. I also knew that I would forever regret watching this man die before my eyes.

There was only one thing to do.

One of us had to jump in and try to save him.

I wasn't about to suggest Alana or Gannon put themselves in harm's way. I would never forgive myself if something happened to one of them. It had to be me.

After a quick assessment of the ocean patterns and rocks, I was convinced that I could make the leap, swim to the man, and pull him to safety.

I stepped to the edge and prepared to jump.

"I'm going in after him," I said, but Alana pulled me back.

"It's too dangerous," she said.

Just then, out of the corner of my eye, I noticed a blur move past me. When I looked down I was shocked. My brother was free falling toward the waves!

Luckily, he timed it well, landing in deep water just as a wave rolled into the cliff. Hitting the surface like a torpedo, he disappeared below the bubbly surf.

I held my breath, waiting for my brother to come up for air.

He didn't.

"I don't see either of them," I said, terrified.

"Neither do I," Alana said.

"Quick, let's get down there!"

I grabbed Gannon's backpack and followed Alana down

the slick and narrow trail to the lava rocks. I was looking for my brother as I ran, and at the same time trying not to slip and fall off the cliff.

We eventually made it to a rock that was just above the reach of the breaking waves. Shielding the sun's glare with my hand, I spotted two heads bobbing in the water not far from us. Gannon actually had the man in his grasp and was trying desperately to drag him to safety.

"There they are!" I shouted. "Let's go help!"

We scrambled over several slippery rocks as waves bombarded the shore, crashing over the top of us as we moved ever closer. When we finally reached them, I could see that the man was unconscious. My brother was doing his best to tread water as he struggled to push the man up onto the rocks. Taking heavy surf head on made this even more difficult. I could tell by the look in Gannon's eyes that he didn't have the stamina to stay afloat much longer.

I got down on my stomach and Alana held my legs so I could reach for them without falling in.

"Grab my hand, Gannon!"

When the next wave lifted them, I was able to grab his arm.

"Hold on tight!"

I used every bit of strength I had to pull Gannon and the man higher on the rock.

"Take him first," Gannon said, gasping.

Gannon pushed the man higher. I let go of my brother

and grabbed the man by his vest. Alana came down and helped grab ahold of him, too.

The waves pounded the rocks.

"I have a good hold," I said, straining.

"Me too," Alana said.

On the count of three, we heaved, pulling the man onto the rocks. His face was blue.

"He's not breathing!" she said, panicked. "I'll try to clear his airway!"

With the man safely on the rocks and Alana providing emergency aid, I turned back to help pull Gannon out of the ocean.

But my brother was gone!

Frantically, I looked around in the surf!

"Gannon!" I screamed at the top of my lungs.

I gasped for breath, as worst-case scenarios flashed though my mind.

Had Gannon been swept away by the waves?

Had he been pulled underwater by the rip current?

Or by a shark?

Each of these tragic scenarios seemed plausible.

I thought about jumping in to search underwater. Problem was, with the strength of these currents, Gannon could have been 50 yards away from me by now.

I ran back along the rocks, slipping and gashing the palm of my hand wide open. Bright red blood flowed from the open wound, but my adrenaline was pumping so hard that I didn't feel any pain. I continued moving over the rocks as fast as I could, desperate for any sign of my brother.

Coming around the cliff's ledge, I looked down into the water. Below me, the ocean swirled like a draining bathtub. Had Gannon been sucked down into it? I had no choice. I had to jump in, and was just about to when I saw his head bobbing on the other side of the pool. He was near a rock that stood a few feet out of the water each time the swell retreated.

"Please pull yourself up there, Gannon," I said as I made my way toward him. "Please!"

That's exactly what he did, dragging himself atop the rock with the very last of his energy. When he made it to the highest point, he rolled over onto his back and didn't move. The next wave tumbled up and over him, moving him closer to the edge. He was so exhausted, he didn't even have the strength to hold on.

With blood streaming from my hand, I maneuvered around the pool toward the rock.

"Hang on, Gannon! I'm coming for you!"

When I made it to my brother, he was unresponsive.

I shook him and called his name.

He didn't wake.

I was terrified he might be dead!

Before I could check his vitals, a big wave nearly took us both out to sea. I swallowed a mouthful of saltwater and was choking as I took my brother under his arms and dragged him to a higher rock, beyond the reach of the waves. Rolling onto his side, he suddenly gurgled, coughed, and spit out lots of water.

"Gannon!" I shouted.

He looked up at me, his eyes only half open. Then he spoke, his voice faint.

"Are you okay?" he said. "You're bleeding."

I never thought I'd say this, but hearing my brother talk was music to my ears!

"Forget about me!" I shouted. "I'm just happy you're alive!"

"Yeah, me too," Gannon said, weakly.

"Next time give me fair warning before you fling yourself into the ocean."

"Where's the man?" he asked. "Is he okay?"

To be honest, I was so worried about my brother I had completely forgotten about the man he had pulled from the sea. When I looked up, Alana was waving us over.

"She might need our help," I said, grabbing Gannon under his arm and helping him to his feet. "Can you walk?"

"I think so. But slowly."

I put Gannon's arm over my shoulder and we followed a longer and safer path back around to Alana. When we got to her, she was holding the man's head in her lap. He was fully clothed, wearing long khaki pants, an oxford shirt and an expedition vest with several pockets. The kind of vest an archeologist would wear in the field. It certainly didn't look like this man had come to the beach to take a swim.

His eyes were opened slightly, and I noticed his stomach rising and falling. Thankfully, Alana had been able to resuscitate the man and he was breathing again.

"He threw up a lot of water," she said. "And I think he might still have some in his lungs."

The man opened his mouth. It looked like he was attempting to speak.

"I think he's trying to tell us something!" I yelled.

Alana put her ear closer to man's mouth. As waves battered the rocks, a salty mist blew over us.

"What's he saying?" I shouted.

"He's speaking Hawaiian! I just can't make it out!"

The man looked to Alana again, desperation in his eyes. She leaned closer when he spoke.

"It's hard to hear," she said, "but it sounds like he's saying *palapala'āina*, which means map!" She leaned in again as the man mumbled. "Yes, that's what he said!"

"Map?" I asked. "What map?"

His hand trembling, the man reached for a pocket in his vest. Too weak to open it, he pointed with a shaky finger and looked to Alana, seeming to request that she remove whatever was inside.

She unfastened the button and reached into his vest pocket. When she withdrew her hand she was holding what looked like a brown document, all wet and about the size of an envelope. The man reached for the paper, and tried to unfold it. Alana helped, spreading it out on the rock beside the man, keeping hold of it to make sure it didn't blow away.

It was a map!

The drawings were slightly distorted by the ocean water, but it was still clear that it was a map of the Big Island. There were symbols and circular diagrams sketched across the top, as well as some words written in what appeared to be the Hawaiian language.

Carefully, I took hold of the map.

"What do you think the map is for?" I shouted over the surf.

The man lifted his head. Alana assisted him.

"Kame . . . ," he said, faintly, pointing at the map. His hand was trembling. "Kameha . . . " His voice was hardly audible over the crashing waves.

"Can you understand him?" Gannon asked.

Alana shook her head and looked into his eyes. The man returned the gaze and gathered what strength he had left.

"Kameha . . . meha," he said.

"Kamehameha?" Alana repeated.

The man nodded, and again pointed to the map. He took a deep breath and spoke again.

"Kamehameha. ʻĀina. Lua pele."

"What's he saying?" I asked.

"It's just random words. He said, 'Kamehameha, land, and volcano.'"

Thinking that the words might not be random at all, but

instead a clue as to what the map was for, I committed them to memory:

Kamehameha, land, volcano.

"Hide," the man said, now speaking in English.

"Hide?" Alana repeated to make sure she heard him correctly.

"Hide," he said, pointing again at the map. "*Maka'u.*"

"What does that mean?" I asked Alana.

"Maka'u means 'danger!'" she said.

"Maka'u," the man repeated.

His eyes fluttered and closed.

We had been able to pull the man out of the water, but his life was still in jeopardy.

"We need to get him to a doctor!" Alana yelled.

How we were going make that happen, I didn't have a clue. It was well over a mile back to the car, with lots of steep terrain to navigate, so carrying him out of the valley wasn't an option.

"Send up a flare!" Gannon shouted.

That's right! We each had an emergency flare in our backpacks.

Quickly, I put the map in my pocket and removed the flare gun. Pointing it over the ocean, I fired. The orange fireball arched high over the water like a blazing comet.

"Hopefully someone will see it and call for help!" Alana hollered, her fingers still pressed against the man's neck to monitor his pulse.

"I'm going to shoot the second flare just in case no one saw the first!" I said, and sent another one soaring up and over the shoreline. On the opposite side of the valley, I spotted two people that had hiked down the trail and onto the beach. I thought maybe they could call for help, so I yelled to them.

"Please help! It's an emergency! We need help!"

I couldn't tell if they heard me over the surf, so I took off running, scrambling over rocks and back across the black sand beach. When I reached the couple, I explained the situation while trying to catch my breath. They dialed 911 several times but because the valley is so remote the call wouldn't go through. Desperate, we climbed some rocks to a higher point, hoping we'd have better luck. By some small miracle it actually worked, the call went through! The dispatcher who answered notified them that someone had seen the flare and the nearest lifeguard station had been notified. A rescue helicopter was already on the way.

Within five minutes a bright orange helicopter flew around the cliffs. Having hiked back to Alana and Gannon, we all started jumping up and down and waving our arms to make sure they saw us. There wasn't room enough to land on the rocks, so instead the helicopter hovered directly overhead at an altitude of no more than a hundred feet. Right away, two climbing ropes unraveled, and two lifeguards repelled to the rocks. Following the lifeguards, a stretcher was lowered to us. One of the lifeguards quickly checked the vital signs of the man we'd pulled from the ocean.

"What's the situation?" the other lifeguard shouted over the sound of the propeller.

"He was drowning in the surf!" Alana said.

"Do you know him?" the lifeguard asked.

"No, we don't!" Alana said, and pointed to my brother, "but Gannon jumped in and rescued him!"

"That was very brave of you, son!" he said. "But you're very lucky you both didn't drown!"

"I studied the currents and the swell before I jumped! I was confident I could save him!"

"Sounds like you're a real waterman!" the lifeguard yelled.

Hawaii's "watermen" are some of the strongest swimmers on earth and have a knowledge of the ocean that is unmatched anywhere. Gannon offered a smile at the compliment.

"We need to get him to the hospital right away!" the other lifeguard shouted.

The lifeguards carefully loaded the man onto the stretcher, strapped him in tight, and signaled the pilots. Slowly and steadily the stretcher was hoisted up and into the helicopter. One of the lifeguards clamped his harness to the rope and was pulled up behind the stretcher. The other lifeguard checked Gannon to make sure he hadn't sustained any serious injuries. Once he'd determined Gannon was okay, he signaled the pilot, who gave a salute, tilted the chopper's nose forward, and flew away.

After cleaning and bandaging my hand, the lifeguard

helped us navigate the steep and jagged shoreline back to the trail.

When we got back to Alana's jeep, we were met by two police officers. They had been sent to write a report of the incident. Still somewhat traumatized by the event, we answered their questions the best we could. One of the officers scribbled away in a small notebook as we talked. Before leaving, word came via police radio that the man had already arrived at the hospital and was listed in critical condition. We were all upset by the news, but the police assured us that the doctors in the intensive care unit were top-notch and would do all they could to save him.

Driving away from the Pololū Valley, the possibility that this man might actually die brought a sick feeling to my stomach. Leaning back against the headrest, I placed my hand on my leg and remembered the map in my pocket. Carefully, I slid it free and held it in my hand.

"I forgot to tell the police about the map," I said.

"That's probably a good thing," Alana said. "It would have just made them ask more questions we don't have answers to. Besides, there's something suspicious about the whole incident. What was that man doing in the ocean, fully clothed and carrying an old map in his pocket?"

"I was thinking the same thing," Gannon said. "It doesn't make much sense."

"We need to talk to someone who knows something about this map before we just hand it over," Alana said.

"Have anyone in mind?" I asked.

"I think my mom might be able to help. She's the historian at Puʻuhonua o Hōnaunau National Historic Park. Hopefully she can tell us something about it."

I slid the map into my backpack, fell into a deep sleep, and didn't wake until we arrived. Right now, we're resting in Alana's mom's office. The plan is to show her the map as soon as she's done giving a tour. I keep wondering what really happened to that man today. Was it just an accident? Had he simply been exploring and fallen into the ocean? It's too soon to know, but my instincts tell me there's a lot more to it.

PART II

A ROYAL MYSTERY

GANNON

O h, man, after today I have a whole new respect for the ocean. In its grasp even the strongest swimmer is helpless. Sure, I tried to put on a brave face after the whole ordeal, but to be honest, when I was being sloshed around in the surf, I was freaking out a little. Okay, a lot. Anyway, right now I barely have the strength to hold this pen, much less write, so I have to keep this journal entry as short as possible.

Soon after we got to Pu'uhonua o Hōnaunau we met up with Alana's mom, Mrs. Aukai. She's a kind and intelligent woman who leads the historical tours at the park. We told her all about the drowning man, about him saying "Kamehameha" and "danger" and giving us the map and how he told us to hide it. Mrs. Aukai was shocked over what had happened, which is totally understandable, but she applauded our bravery and kept saying how thankful she was that we were all okay.

"May I please see the map?" she finally asked.

"Of course," Wyatt said and spread it out on her desk. When Mrs. Aukai saw it, she gasped and put her hand over her mouth, which confirmed to me that we were in possession of something incredibly valuable.

Wooden statues at Puʻuhonua o Hōnaunau

"Are these Hawaiian symbols?" Wyatt asked, pointing to the markings on the map.

"I believe they are," she said. "But I'll need to do some research to find out what they mean." Mrs. Aukai pointed to the corner of the map. "Very faintly here, it appears to read ikiiki. Do you see that?"

Wyatt looked closely.

"I hadn't noticed that."

"Ikiiki is a month in the lunar calendar associated with the summer season."

"That's around the time of year King Kamehameha died," Alana said.

"You're right," Mrs. Aukai said. "Interesting, isn't it?"

"It sure is," Wyatt said.

"What about these circles?" Wyatt asked, pointing to the map. Above the sketch of the island were several circles, each about the size of a baseball, with lots of little black dots inside.

"These circular diagrams could be maps of the stars," Mrs. Aukai said. "See how some dots are bigger than others? Maybe they represent different constellations."

I leaned over the map to get a closer look.

"She's right, Wyatt, look," I said and traced the dots with my finger. "Right here is the Big Dipper and that's probably the North Star in the center. We learned this from Dr. Ward at the observatory, remember?"

"Wow, you're right, Gannon," Wyatt said.

"But what does it mean?" I asked.

"Good question," Alana said.

"Let me pull some books from the library to see what I can find," Mrs. Aukai said. "Until we know more, I think we should keep news of the map quiet. The warning the man gave you worries me."

"Me too," Gannon said.

"So it's agreed?" Mrs. Aukai said, looking at all of us. "We won't mention the map to anyone."

"Agreed," we all said.

Before Alana's mom returned to the office, word of our rescue had spread through the park. Not to pat ourselves on the back or anything, but just about everyone who works here came to the office to introduce themselves and shake our hands and tell us what a brave thing we had done.

Thinking back on the whole experience, I'm not even really sure how it happened. I mean, one minute I'm hiking along the cliff and next thing I know I'm in the ocean trying to save a drowning man. Thing is, I'm a pretty decent swimmer, so maybe it was just one of those times where instinct kicks in and you do something without thinking. One of those times you do something because you have to.

Anyway, at the moment we're closed off in Mrs. Aukai's office with books and files and photographs and other archives spread all over the place. What we're looking for are clues that might help us figure out the actual purpose of this map.

Okay, then. Back to the research.

WYATT

We had just finished going through all of Mrs. Aukai's archives without finding anything related to the map, when someone pounded at the door, startling us all. Between the knocking came a loud voice demanding to be let inside. Immediately, I remembered the warning we'd been given to hide the map, so I slid it from the table and put it in the desk drawer.

When Alana's mom walked over and opened the door, a peculiar-looking man came charging into the office. He was medium height, had a long, narrow face, pronounced cheekbones, and thin dark hair that was parted on the side. Silver-rimmed bifocals sat on the bridge of his nose.

The man introduced himself as Mr. Ichiro Sato from the Smithsonian Institute. Mrs. Aukai said she had seen him around the historic park, but it was clear this was the first time they had met. Mr. Sato went on to explain that he was originally from Tokyo, but had moved to the United States after receiving a master's degree in anthropology from Kyoto University. He was later hired to conduct a study of Hawaii's royal past and oversee the creation of an authentic exhibit at the Smithsonian Museum of American History in Washington, DC. He was also part of a small team of scientists searching for the sacred burial site of King Kamehameha the Great.

"Mr. Sato," I said, and offered my hand. "My name is Wyatt. It's a pleasure to meet you."

We shook.

"We get updates on the progress of your search," Mrs. Aukai said, "but you are the first member of the team I have met personally."

"Well, it's nice to meet you all," Mr. Sato said, "but I have a rather serious matter to address. Very early this morning, a colleague of mine left to investigate an area in the Pololū Valley. He was looking for additional clues that might help lead us to the king's burial site. Against my advice, he went alone. We expected him back hours ago, but he has yet to return."

We all looked at each other. Mr. Sato continued.

"I was just told that earlier today you were involved in the rescue of a man in that area. Is this correct?"

"Yes," I said.

"Was the man you rescued conscious? Did he give you his name?"

"He was in and out of consciousness and mumbling things in Hawaiian," Alana explained, "but we couldn't tell what he was saying."

"Unfortunately, he didn't tell us his name," I added.

"I need you to describe this man," Mr. Sato said. "What did he look like?"

"Okay, uh," Gannon said, and paused. Mr. Sato's aggressive questioning seemed to make him nervous.

"He was Hawaiian," Alana interjected.

"Yeah, maybe around forty years old," Gannon continued. "And he had thick, dark hair that was cut short."

I remembered something about the rescued man that I thought might help.

"He was wearing tan hiking boots," I said, "with cargo pants and an expedition vest."

At that, Mr. Sato took a deep breath.

"It's just as I feared," he said. "I am certain the man you describe is my colleague, Dr. Daniel Makaha."

Again we all looked at one another.

"Where was he taken?" Mr. Sato asked.

"To the Hilo Hospital," I said.

"I have to call at once. Dr. Makaha's family must be notified."

"His family?" Gannon inquired.

"He has a wife and two young daughters."

The thought of his poor family receiving this news brought a lump to my throat.

"Please let us know how he is doing," Gannon said. "I've been really worried about him. We're hoping for the best."

"Thank you for all you did to help. I will make sure his family is aware of your brave deed."

Gannon nodded.

"I'll be leaving very soon for the hospital," Mr. Sato continued, "but before I go I must ask you another important question. You said Dr. Makaha was conscious at times and even speaking."

"Yes," Gannon said. "He was."

"Did he say anything about how he ended up in the ocean? Was it an accident? Was he hiking along the cliff and slipped? I need you to think really hard about this. It's critical that we find out exactly what happened to him."

"He didn't say anything about it," Alana said. "As I said before, he was mumbling in Hawaiian, but we couldn't really hear him over the crashing waves."

"He was *only* speaking Hawaiian? No English?"

"That's right. Just Hawaiian."

Mr. Sato looked at each of us, then asked another question.

"Did he happen to give you anything?"

"What do you mean?" I asked, trying to delay having to answer.

Mr. Sato stared directly at me. His eyes narrowed.

"Dr. Makaha was in possession of something that is very important to our mission," he said.

Given the circumstances under which we found Dr. Makaha, in addition to the warnings he gave us, I was a little skeptical of Mr. Sato. Fact is, I don't know yet who we can trust and don't want to be responsible for the map falling into the wrong hands. Plus, we agreed not to mention the map to anyone until we know more. That said, this was a scientist from the Smithsonian, a very reputable institution. I looked to Mrs. Aukai for guidance. If she felt comfortable showing Mr. Sato the map, then I would be okay with it, too. If she kept quiet about it, I would do the same. I just hoped Gannon didn't start blabbering about it.

"What exactly was he in possession of?" Mrs. Aukai asked.

I glared at Gannon in an effort to silently communicate that he needed to keep his big mouth shut.

"All I can say is that the item has tremendous historical and cultural value," Mr. Sato said.

We all stood silently while he stared at us. I felt a bead of sweat run down my forehead.

"Mr. Sato," Gannon said. "I'll tell you this . . ."

My heart fell into my stomach. My brother was going to tell him about the map!

Gannon continued, "Dr. Makaha was seconds away from drowning when I got to him, and if it weren't for Alana's knowledge of emergency first aid, he wouldn't have survived at all. I'm sure you can understand, given the situation, why we weren't able to have an in-depth conversation with him. I'm sorry, but our goal was to save his life, period."

"That's true," I added, cutting Gannon off. He had succeeded in keeping the map secret, for now, but I know my brother. The more he talks the more likely he is to stick his foot in his mouth. "Hopefully Dr. Makaha will recover. Then he can answer all of your questions."

"We're as curious as you to know how he ended up fighting for his life in that dangerous surf," Alana said.

Mr. Sato glared at each of us.

"Then I will check with the hospital staff as soon as I arrive," Mr. Sato said. "They will have a record of everything Dr. Makaha was in possession of when he was admitted. Thank you for your time."

Before Mr. Sato passed through the door, Mrs. Aukai spoke.

"Excuse me, Mr. Sato," she said. "May I ask you a question before you leave?"

Mr. Sato stopped and turned around.

"Quickly," he said.

"I'm sure you're aware that your search is quite controversial," she continued.

"I am."

"Many fear that the king's bones will be taken to a museum far away and that the site will not be treated with the respect it deserves. So I must ask, what do you intend to do, should you discover this sacred site?"

"Frankly, that's none of your business," he said.

"Jeez, how rude," Gannon said under his breath.

"Excuse me?" Mr. Sato said, turning to Gannon.

"Nothing."

"I have to go now," Mr. Sato said. "My colleague needs me."

At that, he exited through the door, slamming it shut behind him.

Despite Mr. Sato's poor manners, I cannot completely rule out the possibility that his intentions are good. His colleague is in critical condition and he has the responsibility of notifying the man's family. Such a task would put a strain on anyone. That said, I think it was a smart move not to mention the map. Alana's mom agreed.

"I do not want to pass judgment on Mr. Sato after one brief conversation," Mrs. Aukai said. "He may be a good person, but it's a hard to respect someone who does not show you respect in return."

"I'll say," Gannon huffed.

"We know nothing of this man from Washington, DC, and it would not have been wise to hand over a possible cultural treasure to a complete stranger."

"It's good we were all on the same page," Alana said.

"There are a few scientists at the Hawaiian Cultural Preservation Society on the island of Oahu that I know well and trust. I would prefer to hand off the map to them instead of Mr. Sato."

"We're headed over to Oahu at the end of the week and can deliver it personally, if you'd like," Gannon said.

"If we don't find anything in our research, I might take you up on that offer."

As a precaution, we've hidden the map among some books in Mrs. Aukai's office. As I write, Gannon and I are resting in a palm-roofed hut just outside the historic park. There's talk that this is where my brother and I are going to stay for the night. The hut is open air, has a pleasant breeze, and is within earshot the waves. I typically love going to sleep in a place where you can hear the ocean, but after today's experience, the sound of crashing waves is slightly unsettling. To make matter worse, Gannon just reminded me that we're in a tsunami zone.

Even so, the hut looks to be about twenty feet above sea level and the probability of a tidal wave crashing ashore within the next ten hours is infinitesimal. This spot also offers cover should it rain, so I think I'll stay right here tonight.

Time to get some sleep. More tomorrow . . .

GANNON

Alana and her mom returned to the park just after sunrise to rouse us, but I was already awake. Had been for half the night. Couldn't stop thinking about Dr. Makaha.

Wyatt slept under the thatched roof hut even though I tried to convince him to move further up the hill beyond the reach of a tsunami, you know, just in case. But he's stubborn and had a thousand reasons not to, saying that the hut was more comfortable and gave him cover from the rain and that the statistical probability of a tsunami actually hitting this beach while we slept was so slim and blah-ba-dee-blah-blah. Ignoring Wyatt's logic and scientific reasoning, I took my sleeping bag and moved to higher ground.

Anyway, after we were up and had put our sleeping bags

away we all went to Mrs. Aukai's office. She had an idea she wanted to discuss in private. Even with the door shut, she spoke quietly.

"Last night, Alana and I stayed up late going through all of my books," Mrs. Aukai said.

"Did you find anything?" Wyatt asked.

"Unfortunately, we did not," she said, "but we had a thought."

"What was it?" I asked.

"There is a Hawaiian elder I knew well as a child. His name is Kalani. Alana met him many years ago at a ceremony at the seven sacred pools in Hana, Maui. He is a descendant of King Kamehameha's Lieutenant and well versed in Hawaiian history. Kalani is quite old now, and only speaks Hawaiian, but given his background Alana and I think he might know something about the map."

"The challenge will be tracking him down," Alana said.

"How hard could it be?" I asked. "I mean, I know this is called the 'Big Island' and all, but it really isn't *that* big, is it?

"Well, it's big enough that all of the other Hawaiian Islands could fit inside it, almost twice over," Alana said.

"Oh, jeez, that's bigger than I thought."

"As big as it is in comparison to the other islands," Mrs. Aukai added, "you can still drive around the entire island before sundown. What makes this mission difficult is that Kalani has always lived beyond where the roads will take you. Last I knew, his home was a simple hut in the remote Waipi'o Valley.

The people there live much like the old Hawaiians. Many are taro farmers. There is no electricity and there are no phones."

"I like this place already!" I said. "When can we go?"

"We can leave now," Alana said.

"Bring a couple of tents with you," Alana's mom suggested. "Should you find Kalani prepare to stay the night in the valley. I wouldn't advise that you hike out after sundown and I don't know if he will have accommodations for unexpected guests. Also bring my satellite phone, just in case you run into trouble."

I'm packed and ready to hit the road, but before we take off I need to call the Hilo Hospital to check on Dr. Makaha. Fingers crossed he's doing better.

WYATT

FEBRUARY 5, 10:43 AM
74° FAHRENHEIT, 23° CELSIUS

Before we left the historic park, Mrs. Aukai suggested we take steps to protect the map from any further deterioration. The saltwater had caused some damage, but the map held together and most of the markings are still clear enough to see.

Carefully, Mrs. Aukai folded the map and zipped it into a waterproof pouch. I put the pouch into a plastic folder and slid it into my backpack, promising her I would take good care of it. I don't think I would ever forgive myself if the map were ruined while it was in my possession.

A cluster of palms among the lava

Alana and I then went about packing while Gannon called the hospital to get an update on Dr. Makaha. A few minutes later, we all met at the jeep.

"I talked to a nurse at the Hilo Hospital," Gannon said, as he climbed into the backseat. "Unfortunately, Dr. Makaha's condition hasn't improved much. I'll check in again as soon as we get back from the Waipiʻo Valley."

As Alana backed out of the parking lot, someone smacked their hand hard against the passenger side window, causing me to jump in my seat. It was Mr. Sato. He was drenched in sweat, the bangs of his black hair wet and matted to his forehead.

"I'm so glad I caught you," he said, panting.

I rolled down the window.

"Listen," Mr. Sato said. "I just returned from the hospital. Dr. Makaha is still in a coma."

"I just talked to a nurse," Gannon said. "She told me they're still hopeful he'll pull through."

"That's certainly an optimistic outlook. The most likely outcome, however, should he survive, is that he will be severely disabled for the rest of his life."

Devastated by this sad news, we all sat quietly for a moment. Finally, Gannon spoke.

"They didn't say anything about that to me," he said.

"They were sparing you, son. I'm sorry to be the bearer of bad news, but it seems Dr. Makaha suffered severe brain damage from the accident."

Gannon became almost despondent, sinking into the backseat.

"It is possible he may never be able to communicate again," Mr. Sato continued. "That is why your help is so critical."

"What do you mean?" I asked.

"As I told you, Dr. Makaha was in possession of a very important artifact. I checked with the lifeguards and nurses. Other than his clothes, a pocket knife and basic set of archeological tools, they found nothing on him."

I looked over at Alana and noticed her jaw muscles rippling. She was grinding her teeth—a sign, I thought, that she still did not trust Mr. Sato. We all knew what was coming. Mr. Sato was going to try to pressure us into telling him about the map. Unless he had seen Dr. Makaha give us the map, though, there was no way he could know we had it in our possession. Alana's mom was the only other person that knew, and she definitely hadn't told him. He was just speculating that we might have it because it wasn't found on Dr. Makaha.

"Mr. Sato," I said. "We told you yesterday, we don't know what you're talking about. Our focus was to save Dr. Makaha from drowning. Not long after we pulled him from the ocean he was flown to the hospital."

"Isn't it possible that the artifact you're looking for is in the ocean?" Alana said. "If Dr. Makaha had been carrying it, it could have slipped from his hands when he was struggling to stay afloat."

"That's true," I said.

Mr. Sato just stared at us, his left eye twitching.

Alana had given a perfectly logical explanation. Why Mr. Sato wouldn't accept this as a likely scenario was odd to me. It was like he knew something that he wasn't telling us.

Mr. Sato looked around the parking lot, as if to make sure no one else could hear our conversation.

"I have a strong hunch you all know exactly what I'm looking for," Mr. Sato said. "Would that hunch be correct?"

I shook my head "no."

"It's a map," he said, his tone angry, almost sinister.

I felt my heart rate quicken.

"A map that is of no value to you, but of tremendous value to me. I suggest you give it to me, unless you care to deal with the Hawaiian warrior spirits."

Gannon leaned into the front seat.

"What *warrior spirits*?" he asked, his voice shaky.

"Legend has it that the map is protected by the spirits of ancient warriors," he said. "Should it fall into the wrong hands, such as yours, it is believed that the warriors will come to reclaim it."

Though I respect the beliefs of different cultures, being of scientific mind, I simply don't buy into this sort of myth and legend. However, I could see in their eyes that Alana and Gannon were impacted by the story.

"I can't help but feel that the warrior spirits had something to do with Dr. Makaha's accident," Mr. Sato continued. "I am experienced in this line of work and willing to accept such dangers, but I would hate for these horrors to befall youngsters like yourselves."

Mr. Sato was trying to manipulate us. He wanted the map, and was trying to scare us into giving it to him, but that wasn't going to happen.

"Mr. Sato, I'm sorry we couldn't be of more help," I said. "But we have to go. Unfortunately, our time in Hawaii is limited."

"Where are you going?" he asked, sternly.

"I'm taking them on a tour of the island," Alana said.

"Not sure yet if we'll take the north or south route. I'll decide when I get to the main road. We'll be back in a couple days."

I smiled, nodded cordially, and rolled up the window.

As we drove out of the parking lot, Mr. Sato stared at us coldly.

"Why did he have to tell us about the warrior spirits?" Gannon said. "I mean, that's something I really didn't need to know about."

Alana kept quiet, so I did my best to alleviate his fears.

"We'll be fine, Gannon. Just forget he even said it."

"Sorry," Gannon said, "but you know that's not possible."

To review, our plan is as follows: We will try to track down Kalani and see if he can offer some insight into the meaning of the symbols, celestial drawings, and the map. If we can't find him, or he has no information, we will send the map to the scientists in Oahu that Mrs. Aukai trusts. At least then we'll know the map is in good hands. If Mr. Sato wants access to the map at that point, he can work with the scientists at the Hawaiian Cultural Preservation Center, and that's that!

GANNON

En route to the Waipi'o Valley. I'm in the backseat of Alana's jeep, reading a book she brought with her on Hawaiian culture and myth. Just trying to take my mind off Dr. Makaha's tragic situation, but I think this book is only making me more upset. Being the type that totally buys into that sort of stuff, I have to be honest, I'm totally and completely haunted by the idea of warrior spirits. I mean, the beliefs of the indigenous people have been passed down through the ages. Who am I to dispute thousands of years of wisdom?

I just read a section about the "legend of the night marchers" and, well . . . you know what, forget it. It's so freaky, I can't even write about it right now. So, yeah, time to fill my head with other thoughts, good thoughts, and pronto.

Let's see, so, at this very moment we're driving through sporadic forests of eucalyptus and wide open spaces. Out the window I see lava rocks, pink flowers, a farm, cattle, horses, and tall green mountains.

Now we've come to a small town and are driving down the main street. A market, hotels, several little shops, and a theater. On the wall of the post office a sign reads, "Captain Cook, Hawaii 96704."

Obviously this town is named after the famous British explorer, Captain James Cook, who was killed by natives somewhere nearby. That was back in 1779, if I remember correctly. Captain Cook was an incredibly brave and accomplished explorer, one of the greatest actually, though some say he was getting a little pushy with the Hawaiian people and only got what he deserved. You know, I wonder if the warrior spirits had anything to do with the captain's tragic death?

Agh, back on the negative train of thought. And just hit with a little car sickness, too. So, yeah, time to put away the journal and the book, let go of all these nightmarish thoughts and find my happy place.

Come on, G-man.
You can do it.
I know you can.

WYATT

FEBRUARY 5, 7:49 PM
WAIPI'O VALLEY, HAWAII
73° FAHRENHEIT, 23° CELSIUS
PARTLY CLOUDY

Waipi'o Valley from lookout

Hiking into the Waipi'o Valley is like stepping back in time.

Located on the north shore of the island, the interior of
the valley cannot be accessed by car. However, there is a steep

mountain road that winds down to the valley floor. Some claim it is the steepest road in the world. The road is dirt, rutted with potholes and is famous for burning a car's brakes to the point of being useless. Alana told us there have been a number of bad accidents on this road over the years, so I had no objection when she suggested we park at the end of the pavement and hike down.

The view from the ridge was incredibly picturesque. I stopped to take a few photos, while Gannon shot some video. High mountain slopes were draped like emerald curtains on either side of the valley. The valley itself, lush and jungle-like, ran long and flat from the coastline. Along the shore was a black sand beach, the remnants of solid lava broken down over thousands of years by the ocean waves. Using my camera's zoom lens, I scanned the beach and did not see a single person, I assume because it takes such effort to get down to it. Off shore, clouds cast dark circles of shade on the bright blue ocean. Other parts of the Pacific were exposed and sparkling under the sun.

"I just realized something," Gannon said, taking in the view. "The places I like best in Hawaii are the places with no hotels."

Alana smiled. Gannon had a point. The Waipi'o Valley was unspoiled Hawaii at its best. Paradise in the Pacific.

"You know, Mr. Sato had me feeling pretty crummy with his news of Dr. Makaha and all that warrior spirit talk, but just seeing this beautiful valley has totally improved my mood."

"Nature has the power to do that," Alana said. "You both ready?"

"We sure are," I said. "Let's go."

From the ridge, we hiked down the road. A recent rain had muddied the dirt, making certain parts slick. Thick jungle grew over from both sides. About halfway down, we found an abandoned truck that had slid off the road and come to rest upside down in the bushes. More evidence that we made the right choice in leaving the jeep and traveling on foot.

"There are probably less than fifty people living in this valley today," Alana said, as we walked. "They are mostly the descendants of past generations who farmed and lived off the land. Many historians believe this is where King Kamehameha spent much of his childhood. Just look around and you can see why native Hawaiians consider this such a special place."

"I totally get it," Gannon said, stretching his arms wide and spinning around. "I can feel the positive energy."

I rolled my eyes. Gannon noticed.

"Hey, I'm serious, Wyatt! Can't you feel it? It's pulsing from the forest. This place is so alive!"

Gannon walked up to a big tree just off the path.

"What kind of tree is this?" he asked Alana.

"It's a koa tree," she said.

"Get over here, Wyatt."

I indulged him and walked to the tree.

"Now give it a big hug," he said.

"Sorry, Gannon," I said. "I'm not hugging a tree."

"Oh, that's so not cool, bro. For real, what has this tree ever done to you?"

Again I rolled my eyes.

"I'll tell you," Gannon continued. "It hasn't done anything *to* you, but it's definitely done something *for* you."

"What are you talking about?"

"This tree has spent its life absorbing carbon, which makes the air cleaner and healthier for all of us. For that reason alone, I think this tree deserves a big hug. Seriously, bro. It's the least you can do to show your appreciation."

"Go on, Wyatt," Alana said. "You'll be surprised how good it feels."

If it had just been my brother, I would have told him where to stick it, but I wasn't about to say no to Alana.

Reluctantly, I stepped up and put my arms around the tree.

"Ahhhh, there you go, Wyatt," Gannon said. "Give that tree some love."

Gannon walked to the other side and put his arms around the trunk, as well.

"Oh, yeah," he said. "Feel that energy flowing through your body?"

"All I feel is some scratchy bark against my face."

"Oh, stop it. You can't tell me you don't feel the energy. This tree is full of it."

"No, you're full of it," I said. I was done with Gannon's hippie, tree-hugging experiment and wanted to move on.

"Let's keep going. We need to do our best to find Kalani before nightfall."

"Boy, am I feeling good now," Gannon said. "Totally rejuvenated thanks to Mr. Koa."

"You honestly get a little weirder every day," I said.

Gannon just laughed as we continued down the steep switchbacks all the way to the valley floor. I imagined this is what Hawaii must have looked like thousands of years ago. As we walked deeper into the valley, Alana pointed out monkey pod and mango trees, tropical almond, Indian mulberry, and beach naupaka, which have little blossoms that look like flowers cut in half. She also identified a number of bird species. Most of them, just like those in the Pololū Valley, were endangered.

Waterfalls shower the valley from several high places, and Alana insisted we take a short detour and hike to the tallest, Hiʻilawe Falls. It was well worth the extra effort. Gazing up from the pool below, it felt as if we were inside the belly of the earth. High green walls encircled us, while a plume of water fell into a clear pool. The pool's surface rippled in the wind that blew from the falling water, coating our skin with a cool, refreshing mist. Gannon and I had worked up a good sweat and were about to take a swim to freshen up, but reconsidered after Alana warned us of the falling rocks.

"It is dangerous to swim under a waterfall," she said. "If a rock were to fall from the cliff and hit you in the head it could kill you."

"Well, all righty then," Gannon said. "I guess you'll just have to deal with my B-O a little longer."

"Any chance Kalani will have a shower we can use?" I asked, half-joking.

"Yes," Alana said. "The nearest stream."

"That'll work," Gannon said.

Hiʻilawe Falls drops 1,450 feet.

Leaving Hiʻilawe Falls, we came to a high vista that opened up to the lush valley below. I pointed out a few geometric shapes in the valley, and Alana explained that they were taro patches. She thought one of them might belong to Kalani.

Making our way down to the first patch, we were greeted by an old woman in a red flowered dress. She had long, white hair and spoke to Alana in Hawaiian. The woman was very friendly and smiled as she told us that Kalani lived just down the hill.

Walking along the bank of a pebbled stream, we came to a very basic hut set among a forest of immense palm trees.

From inside the hut, an elderly, shirtless man appeared.

"Aloha," Alana said to the man as he approached.

"Aloha," he said, giving us a curious look.

"Kalani?" Alana asked, to which he nodded. "I thought so!" she said, excitement in her voice.

When she explained in Hawaiian that she is the daughter of Mrs. Aukai, a smile spread across the man's face. Kalani gave a simple nod and lifted his arm, welcoming us to his home. Of course, Gannon, the "language expert" of our family, had to try his hand at speaking Hawaiian. The attempt got a good laugh out of the old man.

"What's so funny?" he asked Alana. "I was just trying to say 'we're happy to be here.' Did I mess it up?"

Alana was laughing, too.

"What you said was closer to 'my feet stink.'"

"Oops," Gannon said, and laughed. "Looks like I need a little more practice before I can converse with the locals."

Alana went on to tell Kalani the purpose of our visit. She

told him about Dr. Makaha and the map, his instruction to keep it hidden and warning of danger. All the while, Kalani stood still, his eyes permanently locked on her.

When she finally finished, Kalani offered little response, only saying that the time had come to begin dinner and inviting us to set up camp wherever we would be most comfortable.

I am beginning to wonder if this man, who lives so simply and speaks so little, will be able to tell us anything about the map.

I suppose we'll find out soon enough.

More after dinner . . .

GANNON

A natural shower

Wow, I mean, *WHAT A PLACE!*

Deep in this lush valley with all the palms and the trickling stream and the waterfalls and Kalani's thatched roof hut and the taro field and lava rock fire pit, it's like we've magically entered the realm of the ancient Hawaiians or something. Seriously, if I saw King Kamehameha the Great walk out of the jungle I honestly don't think I'd be surprised.

My nose is telling me that Kalani has started cooking dinner over the fire, but I want to make some quick notes on our campsite. I should begin by saying it's pretty much the most awesome campsite ever. Hanging between two palms is a hammock where Alana says she will sleep. I'm not going to lie, that's actually where I wanted to sleep—outside, under the stars—but hey, ladies' choice, so Wyatt and I ventured up the hill and found a nice, flat section of grass among the trees. As we set up our tent, daylight started to fade. On cue, the singing tree frogs came to life and soon their gurgling cadence echoed through the forest.

"I mean, how awesome is this?" I asked Wyatt, real giddy as we set up our tent. "Seriously, this right here is a true Hawaiian experience. Camping in the valley, bathing in the stream, eating a taro dinner cooked over a fire. We're getting to see exactly how the ancient Hawaiians lived."

"I don't think they had tents and sleeping bags back then, Gannon," my brother said.

"Well, besides that."

Modern camping equipment aside, the Waipiʻo Valley is a place that forces you to disconnect from the rest of the world. There are no TVs or newspapers. No phones or computers. Just you and nature.

"I'm telling you, bro," I continued. "There's a lot we can learn spending time in a place like this. I mean, not only about the culture and history, but about living in general, you know what I'm saying?"

"Not really," Wyatt said.

"Okay, for instance, notice how Kalani sits patiently and listens to every word you say, instead of looking at his phone every few seconds like most people do these days?"

"That's because he doesn't have a phone."

"Right! And I love that! This is the type of place that makes you realize how distracted we've all become with technology. I don't know, I just think it's so refreshing to get away from all that stuff sometimes and simply live in the moment, you know?"

"I agree, Gannon," my brother said. "It really is."

Oh, I hear Alana calling us. Dinner must be ready.

Signing off until morning . . .

Beautiful Hawaiian landscape

WYATT

FEBRUARY 5, 10:52 PM
WAIPI'O VALLEY, HAWAII
70° FAHRENHEIT, 21° CELSIUS
PARTLY CLOUDY

Aglow with flickering candlelight we sat cross-legged on a hand-woven rug outside Kalani's hut. A small fire crackled in a nearby pit. The darkness was alive with noises.

The Waipi'o Valley, we were told by Kalani, is called the "Valley of the Kings" because long ago it was the center of Hawaiian government and religion.

"Just like the Valley of the Kings in Egypt," Gannon said. "Where lots of the pharaohs are buried."

Alana nodded, but did not translate for Kalani, as he was tending to our dinner, using a flat wooden spoon to scoop poi into bowls carved from the trunk of a palm.

If I had to guess, I'd say Kalani's taro patch is 50 ft × 50 ft, or thereabouts. Inside the square plot, heart-shaped leaves rise from a shallow pool of water. Taro is a vegetable that looks similar to a potato. It grows at the base of the root and is used to make poi, a traditional Hawaiian dish. Poi is a pasty, purple substance that looks a lot like blueberry yogurt. This is what Kalani prepared for us tonight, along with some sliced papaya and lime wedges to squeeze over the top.

Without utensils, I wasn't sure how to eat it, so I watched Kalani. What he did was scoop some poi with his pointer and middle fingers, put his fingers into his mouth, close his lips over his fingers and pull them away. It was time to have a go at it, so I cleaned my fingers as best I could and stuck them into the bowl. Scooping a modest amount of poi, I shoved it in my mouth and licked it from my fingers. The sensation of eating off your fingers is a strange one, if you are not accustomed to it, and poi is not the tastiest food in the world. Fact is, poi has hardly any taste at all. Still, I was hungry, and wound up eating all that Kalani gave me, washing each mouthful down with papaya and lime juice.

"Alana, would you ask Kalani if he'd mind telling us about his family's history?" Gannon said.

Alana smiled and spoke to Kalani in Hawaiian. When Kalani responded, Alana translated.

"One of my ancestors was the lieutenant of King Kamehameha the Great. King Kamehameha is the man who unified all of the Hawaiian Islands under one rule. Our family had a close relationship with the royal family for a very long time."

"How long has Kalani lived here?"

Again, Alana translated.

"Most of my life," he said. "The Waipiʻo Valley was a busy place until many decades ago when a tsunami came ashore. It destroyed almost everything."

"Wait a sec," Gannon said. "Did he say tsunami?"

"Yes."

"Was he here when it hit?" Gannon asked.

"Yes," Kalani answered. "I was lucky enough to be on high ground when it struck, so my life was spared. Sadly, many were not as lucky, including members of my family. They were swept away by the surge. After the tsunami very few people remained in the valley. I left, too, but was drawn back years later. This place is too much a part of me. It is one of the few places left in the Hawaiian Islands that has not changed. It is where I was born and where I will die."

The mention of a tsunami had Gannon so nervous he could hardly sit still.

"Um, I have a quick follow up question," Gannon said. "Isn't he worried about another tsunami hitting this valley? Because I am!"

Kalani explained, "I have set up my farm and hut high enough above sea level to protect me from another tsunami. Do not worry. We are safe up here."

"Phew, that's good to hear!"

Kalani asked if we had enjoyed our meal. We all nodded, bowed our heads slightly and thanked him for the food.

"Should we show him the map now?" I asked Alana.

"Sure," Alana said, and then spoke to him in Hawaiian.

I removed the map from my backpack and handed it to him. The flickering light of the fire illuminated the weathered paper as he carefully unfolded it. I watched Kalani study the map. His face held little expression, aside from his eyes. They widened slightly, as if he was seeing something that was of interest to him.

We all waited anxiously as Kalani set the map down in his lap and hunched over it, looking slowly across the paper from one side to the other. After some time, he sat up and spoke softly. Alana continued to translate.

"My father once told me that our ancestor, the lieutenant, had made a map that marked the location of King Kamehameha's sacred burial site. The burial tradition at that time was called *hūnākele*. According to its rules, the burial location of an important person was kept a secret."

My heartbeat accelerated.

Kalani continued, "The map was hidden away so the location would remain unknown except to the few men who laid the king to rest."

"If the site was supposed to be secret, why did they even bother to make a map of it?" I asked.

Alana presented the question to Kalani and translated his answer.

"That is a good question," he replied. "I'm sorry, but I cannot answer for sure. Hawaiians at the time often moved from one part of the island to another. If the king's people moved on, my ancestor, being the king's lieutenant, might have made the map so that he and only he could remember exactly where the remains were left. That, I believe, is why the symbols were etched onto this map. They could be clues, so that if the map was discovered by others, they would still have difficulty finding the location."

"Can Kalani translate the clues?" I asked.

Alana presented the question to him.

Kalani shook his head.

"I do not think so," he said softly, and set the map aside.

I was tingling with excitement over the fact that the map might actually mark the location of the king's burial site, but if Kalani couldn't translate the symbols the map would be useless to us. I resolved to turn over the map to Alana's mom so she could send it to the scientists she knew in Oahu. Sadly, at that point, we'd no longer be involved in the quest to discover the king.

Finished with dinner, we all went to the stream and washed our bowls. Kalani disappeared into his hut and we were about to call it a night when he suddenly returned to the fire pit. He stood quietly for a moment, the firelight flickering against his skin, then asked Alana to translate a question he had for us.

"Before I say goodnight," Kalani said. "I must know what you plan to do with the map?"

We all looked at one another.

"Well," I said, "since we don't know what to make of the symbols, there's really nothing more we can do with the map personally, so we'll most likely send it to a group of scientists in Honolulu and let them study it. But if you're willing to make even a guess that might point us in the right direction, I thought that maybe we would investigate ourselves."

After Alana translated, Kalani looked at me skeptically. I understood why. He had no reason to trust us, just as we had no reason to trust Mr. Sato.

"Of course, Alana would be our guide," I continued. "Please know that we have the utmost respect for the people, culture, and environment of Hawaii. If we were to find the king's burial site, or anything of cultural value, we would handle it with the greatest care."

When Alana finished translating Kalani said nothing. He just stood there staring at each of us for some time as if, with his silent gaze, he could determine our true character and whether or not he could trust us.

Eventually, Kalani sat down and spread the map out in front of him, again eyeing it without expression.

I held my breath, thinking that maybe something had clicked in Kalani's mind. That maybe a spark of memory had cast a light on some forgotten knowledge about the map. His decision now was whether or not to share that information with us.

I prompted him with a question.

"Does he recognize something on the map?"

Alana asked Kalani.

"Before I speak of the map, I must warn you," Kalani said. "The location of the king's bones is a very serious matter. If the location becomes known, news will spread throughout the world. It is critical that good people step in immediately and protect the sacred site and the land around it."

"I'm just curious," Gannon said to Alana. "What does Kalani think will happen if someone were to remove the bones and send them to the museum somewhere far away?"

Alana offered the question to Kalani and translated his answer.

"If the king's bones are moved from the burial site," Kalani said, "it will not only upset many Hawaiians, it could also set off a storm of spiritual unrest."

"Okay, see what I mean?" Gannon shouted. "Kalani said it himself. If we go searching for the king, we could set off a storm of spiritual unrest! Not a thunderstorm, or even a tropical storm, I mean, those I can deal with. He said a spiritual storm . . . and that's a storm I want no part of!"

"That won't happen if *we* discover the site," I said. "We'll make sure it's protected."

"I'd rather not take the chance," Gannon said.

My brother is as superstitious as they come, so its no surprise Kalani's warning scared him.

"Alana," I said. "Please make sure Kalani understands that we'd never do anything against the wishes of the Hawaiian people. On the contrary, we'd do everything in our power to preserve the site."

After Alana translated, Kalani stared at me. His gaze was unexpressive, and at the same time so powerful it held me in something of a trance.

Because we were with Alana and had been sent by Mrs. Aukai, who Kalani knew and respected, my hope was that he would trust our sincerity and be willing to pass on whatever knowledge he held. With just a little more information, some guidance, just a few clues even, we would be able set off on an adventure of the highest order!

Kalani looked back to the map. Again he stared. The suspense was killing me. After a couple minutes, he pointed to a symbol and spoke.

"This, I believe, is Kīlauea," he said. "And here, the sea. This point might represent where Kīlauea meets the sea. Here is the place on the map. It is near Volcanoes National Park."

He was doing it! He was passing on his knowledge to us! I scooped up my backpack and stepped closer, not wanting to miss a word.

Kalani continued.

"This sketch looks like a cove that is near where Kīlauea meets the sea. And I would take note of this marking at the central point of the cove's beach. It may have meaning."

I reached into my backpack, grabbed my journal and started to write as Alana translated Kalani's words.

"What about the circles?" I asked.

"Inside these circles are drawings of the stars as they appear in the sky at different times of the year."

"Just as we thought," Alana said, excitement in her voice.

"Ancient Polynesians used the stars to navigate when they were at sea," Kalani said. "The North Star is especially important, because it does not rotate in the sky as the earth turns. It remains in the same place, directly over the North Pole."

"Right, when we were at the observatory Dr. Ward explained that the stars move around the North Star counterclockwise," I added.

"But how does this help us figure out what this map is all about?" Gannon asked.

As Alana translated, I looked to Kalani, who nonchalantly shrugged his shoulders and pointed to the next symbol.

"This symbol here might be a wave," he said. "You see, and this would be the wave's crest."

Then he put his finger on a geometric shape with many sides and angles. It had straight lines coming off it in all directions.

"This might be a gem of some kind," he said. "But I do not know for sure."

I was writing down everything Kalani said. Again, he reminded us that these were just guesses and that he could very well be wrong.

"I'll say it again," Gannon said, "even if Kalani is right, how are we supposed to figure out what all of it means? It just sounds like a bunch of random things to me."

"I think it's safe to assume that they're clues to the location of King Kamehameha's burial site," I said.

"I agree," Alana said.

"I'll be honest," Gannon said, "I don't think I want to know the king's location. I mean, if we discover his final resting place that might upset the spirits and I'm not up for messing with any spirits and setting off a storm of unrest or whatever. Maybe we should just bring this map back to your mom, Alana, let her send it to the scientists in Oahu and wipe our hands clean of the whole thing."

"That's always an option," I said. "But now that we have some clues, we might be able to make some sense of the map."

"So you're saying you actually want to go search for the king?"

"I think we have to," I said. "Chances are someone will find him eventually. And what if that person doesn't have the best intentions. They might take the king's bones, stuff them in a bag and bring them on tour around the world. They could end up in a warehouse in Washington, DC, or

Tokyo, or sold on the black market to some eccentric collector. Who knows? But if we find the sacred burial site, we can help protect it."

"Or get ourselves cursed by spirits," Gannon said. "Or worse, get ourselves killed! Think about it for a sec. Dr. Makaha was probably using the map for the same purpose, to try to find the burial site, right?"

"I'm sure he was," I said.

"Well, maybe someone or something didn't want him to find it. And that's why he ended up in the ocean."

"So, you believe he was actually thrown into the ocean on purpose?" I asked.

"I don't know. I mean, it's possible."

"He could have just slipped off the cliff's edge."

"True, but we all agree it's a little suspicious. All I know is that I don't want us to be next!"

I turned to Alana.

"Can you please ask Kalani what he thinks we should do," I said.

After Alana asked him, Kalani put his hand to his chest.

"If your heart is pure, *pono* will guide you," he said. "Pono means righteousness. It's doing what's right for you, for others, and for the earth."

"Okay, but how do we know what's right?" Gannon asked.

Alana offered up the question.

Kalani sat back in thought, then spoke.

"Go to the source of the islands," he said, and pointed

again to the symbol on the map he had translated as Kīlauea. "Find this place and look to the stars. It is there, I believe, that you will find an answer."

"How?"

Kalani lifted his arms to the sky.

"It will come to you," he said.

To go to a volcano and wait for an answer to magically appear did not seem very helpful to me. Fact is, I was hoping for some more definitive advice. Advice that was logical and specific. That said, Kalani had graciously passed along all of his thoughts on the map, and he did believe one of the symbols represented Kīlauea. I suppose, then, it's as good a place as any to begin our search.

"If you wish to take Kalani's advice," Alana said, "we can go there tomorrow morning."

"I don't know," Gannon said. "What do you think, Wyatt?"

"We have to go," I said.

"I figured you'd say that."

"Then it's settled," Alana said. "Tomorrow we go to Kīlauea."

The fire faded to embers and the darkness grew more intense around us. Finally Kalani stood, bowed goodnight and walked slowly into his hut. Alana retired to the hammock, and we hiked up the hill to our tent. Before I had finished cleaning the cut on my hand and rewrapping it with a fresh bandage, Gannon was asleep. For the past hour, I've been awake and writing by flashlight. It's now well after midnight, and I should really get some rest. Tomorrow is a very important day.

GANNON

Fast asleep and snug inside our tent, I was unexpectedly jolted awake.

I sat up.

I was breathing heavily.

My heart was going a mile a minute.

I wondered if I'd just had a bad dream or something.

No, it wasn't that. It was something else. Something wasn't right.

I tried to quiet my breathing. I listened. Over the hum of the valley's insects and frogs and the distant "shhhh" of the waterfall, I suddenly heard a sound. A sound that did not belong. As best as I can describe it, the sound was like two river rocks being knocked together—*"clack, clack, clack!"*

I lit the time on my explorer watch.

It was 3:17 a.m.

I mean, who the heck would be outside making noise at this hour? Especially in a place as remote as this!

Wyatt was dead asleep, and I have to be honest, I was super jealous. Oh, man, do I hate it when I'm up and scared in the middle of the night. Especially when I'm the only one awake. Knowing it's much easier to cope with fear when you have someone to share it with, I gave Wyatt a jab in the arm. He didn't even flinch, so I shook him. Still, he didn't move.

The clacking grew louder. It seemed to be getting closer to our tent. I turned on my flashlight, and shook Wyatt again.

"Wyatt," I said. "Get up!"

"Agh," he groaned, and rolled over. "You better have a good reason for waking me up."

"Someone is outside and they're headed for our tent! How's that for a good reason?"

"What?" he said and sat up. "Are you sure?"

"Sure I'm sure. They're banging rocks together or something. It's almost like they want us to know they're coming."

We both listened.

"I don't hear anything," Wyatt said.

"Give it another minute."

We waited longer. Still, there was no rock banging. The silence was eerie.

"I'm going back to sleep," Wyatt said. "There's nothing out there."

"I promise I heard something!" I said.

"It's just your imagination, Gannon. You always get freaked out when we're camping. I swear, next time I'm going to sleep in my own tent."

Wyatt laid back down and closed his eyes. I was really starting to think that maybe Wyatt was right, maybe it was my imagination. But then I heard it again!

Clack, clack, clack!

Wyatt sat up like a shot, his eyes open wide.

"See, I told you!" I said.

Someone was closing in on us. But who?

I could hear footsteps, the rustling of leaves and the snapping of twigs.

"There aren't any large animals in this valley, are there?" I asked.

"It could be a Polynesian boar," Wyatt said. "I read they can weigh up to 150 pounds and have six-inch tusks."

"Seriously?"

"Seriously."

I listened again.

"Those footsteps don't sound like a wild boar to me," I said. "They sound like the two-legged variety."

Listening closely, we tuned into the sound of slow, methodic footsteps moving over the jungle floor. One, followed by another, followed by another.

"That's definitely a person," I said.

"I think you're right," Wyatt said.

"Hello?" I said loudly.

"Kalani, Alana, is that you?" Wyatt hollered.

"Why would they be awake and walking around at this hour?"

"Why would anybody?"

"Right, that's what worries me."

We heard it again. This time it was real loud.

CLACK, CLACK, CLACK!

"That's really close," Wyatt said quietly.

"I'm totally freaked out right now," I whispered. "What if it's a night marcher?"

"A night marcher? What's that?"

"Night marchers are the spirits of ancient warriors. I read about them on our drive today. They come out at night and march across the island."

"Oh, come on, Gannon," my brother said.

"It's true. And when they're on the march, you're not supposed to get in their way or else."

"Or else what?"

"Or else this," I said, and swiped my finger under my throat.

"Oh, please. That's just a myth."

CLACK-CLACK-CLACK!

I turned to Wyatt and spoke as quietly as possible.

"Whoever's making that noise is right outside our tent. What if it's the spirit of King Kamehameha? Maybe he's come for the map!"

"Stop it, already," Wyatt whispered.

"I think we should put the map outside on the rocks."

"No way."

In the light of the moon I could have sworn I saw a shadow move across the wall of the canvas tent. I pointed outside then put my finger over my lips, signaling Wyatt to keep quiet.

There was another "clacking" of rocks, this one louder than any before it.

At any moment I expected the spirit of a tribal chief or

King Kamehameha himself to rip through the tent, point a spear at us, and demand the map!

Then, as mysteriously as the sounds had started, they stopped.

Silence returned to the forest.

A silence that had weight and density to it.

I couldn't relax, and slept with one eye open the rest of the night, which of course means that I didn't really sleep at all. I just laid there in my sleeping bag, haunted by images of warrior spirits wandering around outside our tent.

* * *

By the time the sun's first rays lit the walls of the tent and the birds began to sing their sunrise songs, my eyes were stinging like someone had doused them with hot sauce. But, oh man, what a relief it was to know that morning had finally come. We'd survived the night!

I was so ready to get out of that tent, but as soon as I unzipped the door a disturbing sight froze me in my tracks. About ten feet from us, someone had erected several small towers of stones.

"Wyatt," I said, smacking him on the leg, "you have to see this."

Wyatt sat up and peeked his head through the door.

"Hmm, I don't remember those being there last night," he said.

"That's because they weren't there last night!"

"Well, this sure is interesting."

"Interesting? Uh-uh, Wyatt. Interesting isn't the word. It's just plain freaky is what it is! I'm serious, someone or something is after the map! I swear, if it were up to me, I'd fling that thing into the ocean and let the Hawaiian Gods sort it out. Or at least hand it off to Alana's mom. Heck, at this point, I'd even be happy to pass it off to Mr. Sato. I know he's arrogant and impolite and all that, but I'm sure he and his scientist buddies from the Smithsonian are totally qualified to handle this kind of stuff. We, on the other hand, are not."

Unfortunately, I couldn't talk my stubborn brother into giving up the map. He's still insisting we do some more investigating ourselves and Alana agrees with him, so I guess I'm outvoted. We're packing up soon and hiking out of the valley. Alana and Wyatt want us all to go to Kīlauea in Volcanoes National Park, but I seriously don't know if I'm up for it. Last night rocked my nerves big-time. Okay, true, I'm sleep deprived and a bit loopy and hungry for something other than poi, but I think if we hold onto this map and go about our own investigation, we're asking for some serious trouble, the *spiritual unrest* kind, and as I told Wyatt and Alana, that's the kind of trouble I can do without.

WYATT

Not long after sunrise, we packed our camping gear, offered a grateful farewell to Kalani, and, leaving no trace, hiked out of the Waipi'o Valley. As hard as I tried, I could not convince Gannon to join us. The strange events that took place last night really shook him. He is on a bus to the Hilo Hospital to visit Dr. Makaha, before heading back to the historic park to connect with Alana's mom. Gannon actually believes we may have set off a curse and that the spirits are now after the map.

Alana said we will need this afternoon and tomorrow morning to conduct a thorough exploration of Volcanoes National Park. She and I will be camping somewhere in the park tonight, so the plan is to meet Gannon and Mrs. Aukai back at her office tomorrow night. There's something wrong with the satellite phone, it won't even power up, so Gannon is going to let Alana's mom know the plan. Once we're all back together, we'll discuss what we have learned and move forward from there.

This mission of ours is ambitious. Using the clues Kalani gave us, we're hoping to make headway on, or possibly even solve, Hawaii's great royal mystery! A tall order, for sure, but worthy of our best effort. Worthy for its historical importance. Worthy for its cultural value. Worthy because the king's burial site deserves to be protected.

I must admit, I am hopeful, but I suppose I shouldn't get ahead of myself. One step at a time.

Off to Volcanoes National Park!

PART III

PROTECTING THE KING'S MANA

GANNON

The man I rescued, Dr. Daniel Makaha, was born in the town of Hanalei on the northern most Hawaiian island, Kauai. He has a wife, Anna, and two daughters, Mala and Maria, ages eight and eleven. They are all here at the Hilo Hospital, hoping and praying that he survives.

When I was introduced to the Makaha family, Anna burst into tears and gave me a big hug while thanking me profusely. I had to fight back tears myself, and told her what I did was nothing, that I'm sure Dr. Makaha would have done the same for me if I had been in his situation. Mrs. Makaha's daughters are sweet and polite, though I could see the sadness in their eyes. They're scared, not knowing whether their dad is going to live or die. To deal with such a thing at their age must be incredibly difficult. Honestly, my heart aches for them.

A nurse came and offered to take the girls for a snack in the cafeteria so Mrs. Makaha and I could talk. We sat in the hospital room near a window that offered a view of a green lawn and palm trees. Outside, a crew of landscapers was mowing the grass and trimming back the trees. Watching the men, hard at work in the bright sunshine, then turning back to see Dr. Makaha lying motionless on the bed, I was struck at how life's tragedies coexist with life's routine.

"What does Dr. Makaha do for a living?" I asked.

"My husband is a cultural anthropologist. He has a PhD from Stanford University, with a specialization in Polynesian history."

I nodded, as Mrs. Makaha went on.

"We now live in Oahu. Daniel teaches at the University of Hawaii. When he's not teaching students, he devotes much of his spare time to a personal project he has become obsessed with."

"If you don't mind my asking, what is this personal project?"

"For several years now Daniel's been trying to locate the sacred burial site of King Kamehameha the Great. He believes the king's bones lie hidden somewhere on the Big Island and it's important to him to find and protect this sacred site for the sake of Hawaiian heritage. Based on the evidence he's collected over the years, he's narrowed his search to a couple specific areas."

"What exactly does he want to protect the site from?" I asked.

"There's a group of developers who want to build a resort hotel in one of these areas. At Daniel's request, the Hawaiian government has granted him more time to continue his work, and that's prevented the developers from being able to buy the land. This, of course, has made many of the businessmen very upset."

"Can't they pick another spot to build their hotel?"

"This is one of the most beautiful locations in all of Hawaii. It lies very near Volcanoes National Park. There is a gorgeous white sand beach, towering cliffs of lava rock, and a vibrant reef just offshore. The developers desperately want this property and seem determined to get it at any cost."

Hearing this sent chills down my spine.

"What do you mean by that?"

Mrs. Makaha's eyes again filled with tears.

"Over the past few months, Daniel has received several threats."

"What kind of threats?"

"Anonymous phone calls and untraceable letters."

"What did they say?"

"That he would be smart to give up his search and go back to Oahu. Not much more than that. They were vague, but frightening."

"I'm sorry to have to ask, but I need to know your honest

opinion. Do you think what happened to your husband was an accident?"

Mrs. Makaha was choked up.

"I cannot say for sure," she whispered, her eyes glassy, "it certainly could have been. His search for clues has taken him to some dangerous parts of the island."

Mrs. Makaha leaned in close and spoke so quietly I could hardly hear her.

"But I must tell you," she said, "I would not be surprised if there was foul play involved."

"Mrs. Makaha," I said, also speaking in a whisper, "your husband gave us a very old map. Do you know anything about it?"

"A map? No, I don't."

"Last night, a descendant of King Kamehameha's Lieutenant told us what he could about the map. There's a possibility it could pinpoint the King's final resting place."

"Do you still have it?" she asked.

"We do. Dr. Makaha told us to hide it. It's with my brother right now, but we could bring it to you."

"My husband gave it to you for a reason. For safekeeping, I assume. You risked your life to save his, so obviously he trusted you. I think you should keep it until he recovers. Does anyone else know you have it?"

"I don't think so, but I can't say for sure."

"Please be careful, Gannon. The fact that my husband told you to hide the map means that other people must be after it."

"When he wakes up," I said, "please tell him we'll keep it safe and promise to return it to him as soon as he's better."

As I handed Mrs. Makaha a tissue to wipe her tears, a thought came to me: If Dr. Makaha's accident was the result of foul play, the person responsible might be the same person that was trying to scare us in the Waipi'o Valley. I've thought all along that we might get ourselves into trouble by holding onto the map, but if we're dealing with people who are willing to kill for it, the situation is much worse than I thought.

I turned to Dr. Makaha. He looked so frail. His cheeks were sunken, his skin nearly bleached of color. I almost couldn't bring myself to admit it, but he appeared close to death. The only indication that there was any life left in him was the monitor that tracked his pulse with a faint, rhythmic beep.

"Has he improved at all?" I asked.

"His condition improved slightly last night, but not since," Mrs. Makaha said.

The nurse returned with Mala and Maria. Mrs. Makaha took both of her daughters into her arms. She looked like she was about to fall to pieces, and I wouldn't have blamed her, but each time I thought she might break down, she took a deep breath and maintained a brave face for her children.

Before leaving the room, the nurse informed us that they had requested Dr. Makaha be transferred to Honolulu. Hawaii's capital, Honolulu is by far the largest city in the state. There is an excellent hospital there with a top-rated trauma unit that will be able to provide the best care available.

In an effort to take their mind off the situation for a bit, I engaged Mala and Maria in conversation, asking them all about their school in Honolulu. They were telling me about the teachers and what they were learning when Mrs. Makaha gasped! I turned around and was shocked to see Dr. Makaha's eyes partially open. His wife took his hand and squeezed it.

"Daniel! It's me! Anna!"

Mala and Maria ran to their dad's bedside.

"Daddy!" Mala shouted, her eyes filling with tears.

When Dr. Makaha looked his wife in the eyes, she began to weep with joy.

"Hi, Daddy," Maria said, leaning over the bed and resting her head on his chest.

I ran to the door.

"Nurse!" I shouted down the hall. "Quick! Dr. Makaha is conscious!"

I moved back to his bedside. Dr. Makaha's eyes were drifting. He seemed to be in a daze.

"Daniel, can you hear me?" his wife asked.

He nodded weakly.

"The nurse is coming," I said to Mrs. Makaha.

His eyes closed and opened again. As he looked around the room, he suddenly noticed me standing behind his wife and kids. Right away his eyes widened and he reached out.

"What is it, dear?" Mrs. Makaha said.

Dr. Makaha was pointing at me, so I moved closer. When

I did, he grabbed my arm. I could feel his hand trembling as he tried to speak. I lowered my ear toward his mouth and he mumbled something in Hawaiian, just as he had when we rescued him from the ocean.

"He's speaking in Hawaiian," I said to his wife. "But I don't know the language very well at all. Do you?"

"Unfortunately, I don't. Daniel is the only one in the family who speaks Hawaiian."

The nurse walked briskly into the room and stepped to his bed.

"Hello, Dr. Makaha," said the nurse. "You're at the Hilo Hospital. Later today we are transporting you to Honolulu. They will take great care of you there."

He seemed to pay no attention to the nurse, and instead kept his eyes locked on me. I felt like he wanted to say something else, so I leaned in. Again, he whispered some words that I didn't understand.

"Do you know Hawaiian?" I asked the nurse.

"No, I don't."

"Daniel, what are you trying to say?" Mrs. Makaha asked. "Can you tell us in English?"

For whatever reason, he continued to mumble in Hawaiian.

"The day we rescued him he was mostly speaking Hawaiian, too," I explained.

"That's strange," Mrs. Makaha said.

"It could be a result of the brain trauma he suffered

during his accident," the nurse said. "Such a shock can certainly affect a person's speech."

Quickly, I stepped to my backpack, removed my journal, and ran back to Dr. Makaha's bedside.

His eyelids were fluttering.

"Stay with us, Daniel," Mrs. Makaha said.

"Dr. Makaha, can you please repeat what you were saying?" I asked.

He took a deep, wheezing breath, then spoke.

"Kamehameha. 'Āina. Lua pele."

I scribbled the words as fast as I could.

"I'm pretty sure that's the same thing he said after we pulled him from the ocean," I said. "If it is, it means 'Kamehameha, land, volcano.' Do you have any idea why he'd be telling us these things?"

"I'm sorry, I don't," Mrs. Makaha said.

But Dr. Makaha wasn't done speaking.

"Saaaa . . . " he said, his voice trailing off.

"What was that?" I asked, pen and journal still in hand.

"Saaaa-to."

"Sato?" I asked, wanting to be sure I'd heard him correctly.

He nodded.

"Mr. Sato, the scientist?"

Again, he confirmed with a nod.

"He was here for a short time yesterday," Mrs. Makaha said.

"Yes, I remember him," the nurse said. "He asked to see

everything that Dr. Makaha had on him when the lifeguards brought him in. He was looking for something, but didn't say what."

Mrs. Makaha looked at me. We were both thinking the same thing. Mr. Sato was looking for the map.

"What about Mr. Sato?" I asked Dr. Makaha. "Do you want us to contact him for you?"

Dr. Makaha shook his head "no."

"E maka'ala iā ia o kā'ili 'ia ka 'āina," he said.

He spoke slowly and repeated what he had said a second time, seeming determined that I get it all. Again, I scribbled down every word, spelling what he said the best I could. When I looked back to Dr. Makaha his eyes were again closed and he was taking rapid, shallow breaths.

I glanced at the nurse, who was reading the monitor above the bed. Without warning, the monitor, which had continued at a steady beep since I'd entered the room, emitted a solid tone. I'm no doctor, but to me it sounded like a flat line!

"What's happening?" Mrs. Makaha asked the nurse. "Is he okay?"

"That tone indicates that his blood pressure has risen to a dangerously high level," she said, nervously.

"I'll get the doctor," I said and took off running.

Way down the hall I spotted an emergency room doctor in a white coat. I sprinted down the hall to him, explained the situation, and we both ran back to the room. Mrs. Makaha had both arms around her daughters and was doing her best to keep her composure. Moving quickly, the doctor and nurse administered some medicine into his IV. Whatever they gave him worked like a miracle, stabilizing his blood pressure almost immediately. The solid tone stopped.

"He's stabilizing," the doctor said.

Wow, did we all breathe a huge sigh of relief!

"His heartbeat has been erratic, putting him at risk of cardiac arrest," the Doctor continued. "The doctors at the Honolulu ICU are better equipped to handle the situation if something goes wrong. I am going to call and increase the urgency of his helicopter transport. The sooner we get him there, the better. Mrs. Makaha, you and your daughters can ride along if you wish."

"We will, thank you," she said, still comforting her daughters.

Before leaving I gave Mrs. Makaha another hug. Again, she told me to be extremely careful. I assured her that I would and promised I'd call her in Honolulu tomorrow to check on her husband. In a situation like this, it's hard to come up with just the right thing to say. We both knew the situation was grave, yet I wanted to say something positive, and that made me feel like whatever words I chose, no matter how heartfelt, would have no real truth to them.

"He's going to pull through," I said to her, trying my best to hide my concern. "You watch, before long he'll be home and life will be back to normal."

Wiping her tears, she smiled.

"Thank you, Gannon," she said. "You're right. Daniel is strong and I have faith he will recover."

That's it, I thought. There's really only one thing you can do when faced with a tragedy, and that is to have faith.

I stepped outside into a warm sun shower. Big drops darkened the hot gray asphalt. Steam rose from the ground in a wavy mist. I could feel the warmth of the steam against my legs, and smell the road's musty, tar scent. I looked up into the sky, hoping to spot a rainbow or any hopeful sign. I couldn't find one.

On the other side of the parking lot, I came to the covered bench where I was told to wait for the bus that will take me back over Saddle Road to Puʻuhonua o Hōnaunau National Historic Park. As soon as I get there, I'll find Alana's mom and ask her to translate the message from Dr. Makaha. The fact that he mentioned Mr. Sato makes me wonder: Was Dr. Makaha trying to tell me that Mr. Sato could help, or was he trying to warn me about him?

WYATT

```
1:12 PM
VOLCANO HOUSE   19° 25' N   155° 15' W
ELEVATION: 4,049 FT.
```

The Volcano House resembles the type of classic mountain lodge you might see in Yellowstone or Yosemite. The hotel itself is built on the very edge of an active volcanic vent, or caldera. Lush ferns and other vegetation grow abundant along the cliff's edge. Beyond the greenery, the landscape drops off and changes dramatically. Charred black rock stretches toward the horizon, like an ashy pool, encircled by high green walls. Hissing plumes of smoke rise from the crater. It looks as if the earth had one day simply collapsed upon itself.

Caldera view from Volcano House

Somewhere below the volcanic haze, bright red lava was bubbling up from deep underground. To see this, an actual river of molten lava, is one of the things I have been looking forward to most. Tonight, I'm hoping we'll get the chance.

The interior of the Volcano House has high wood-beamed ceilings and a huge stone fireplace with Pele the Fire Goddess carved into the chimney rocks. At the back of the hotel are walls of windows and a deck of rocking chairs overlooking the smoldering Kīlauea caldera.

Both hungry, Alana and I stopped for a snack at the hotel's restaurant, The Rim.

"I can't imagine there are many restaurants in the world with a view like this," I said, as I munched on macadamia nuts and rainbow papaya.

"It is unique, that's for sure," Alana said.

Walking back through the lobby, I could smell the scorched earth, probably forever embedded in the walls and carpeting of the lodge. Alana went to register our names with the park rangers and get the latest volcanic activity report. I have taken a seat near the fireplace and am thumbing through *Mark Twain: Roughing it in the Sandwich Islands*, a collection of newspaper columns he wrote in the 1860s. It's almost hard to believe that these islands were ever called the Sandwich Islands. Captain James Cook gave them the name in 1778, in honor of England's Earl of Sandwich. As Mark Twain wrote, "Why did not Captain Cook have taste enough to call his great discovery the Rainbow Islands?" Mr. Twain, I couldn't agree more. When King Kamehameha the Great united the islands under one rule, the official name became the "Kingdom of Hawaii."

Seated here, listening to the wood crackle in the fireplace,

I continue to think about all of the clues we've gathered. Here's what we have so far:

```
Star formations at different times of year
King Kamehameha, the land, and volcano
The place where Kilauea meets the sea
A cove and a central point on the beach
A wave or a wave's crest
And a gem of some kind
```

Problem is, Alana and I can't figure out how in the world these clues might all tie together. Hopefully, it will start to make sense once we're there, but it's also possible we'll still be just as confused as we are now.

Kalani said to go to the source of the islands and look to the stars, and despite the dangers of trekking through an area that is volcanically active, this is what we must do.

Alana's back, so it's time to go.

More tomorrow . . .

Pele carving in the fireplace

GANNON

Arriving at the historic park, I found Alana's mom in her office. She had just finished giving a tour.

"Hello, Gannon," she said excitedly. "Did you find Kalani?"

"We did, actually."

"Oh, my. That's exciting. Was he able to tell you anything about the map?"

"Well, based on its condition, he thought it might have been made by his ancestor, the lieutenant."

"Just as I suspected!" Mrs. Aukai shouted. "Did he say for what purpose?"

"He thinks it might show where the king was laid to rest."

"So our hunch was correct?"

"According to Kalani, it could be."

"That's just amazing, Gannon!"

"He wasn't completely sure about the symbols, but he told us what he thought each one might mean."

"I knew Kalani would be able to help!"

"After we left the valley, I went to the Hilo Hospital to see Dr. Makaha."

"How is he doing?"

"To be honest, there hasn't been much of a change in his condition, but he's hanging in there. Just in case things get worse, the doctors are flying him to Honolulu where he can get better treatment."

"I was hoping for better news," Mrs. Aukai said.

"Me too. But while I was at the hospital, he regained consciousness for a couple minutes and said a few more words in Hawaiian. I thought maybe you could translate?"

I grabbed my journal and put it on the desk.

"Sure, let me take a look," she said.

"First he said Kamehameha, 'āina, lua pele, which is the same thing he said the day we rescued him."

"Right. Kamehameha, land, and volcano."

"Yes, but then he said this."

I flipped to the page and pointed to the new words I'd written down. Alana's mom took a pen, added appropriate markings and signs to the words, then read it aloud.

"E maka'ala iā ia o kā'ili 'ia ka 'āina."

"What's it mean?" I asked.

"Maka'ala means *beware*," she said.

"And the rest?"

"The literal translation is 'beware of him or the land will be taken.'"

A feeling of panic came over me.

"He was trying to warn us," I said to myself.

"Warn you of what?"

"I think he's trying to warn us about Mr. Sato."

Mrs. Aukai covered her mouth with her hand.

"Dr. Makaha mentioned his name several times. I thought that maybe he wanted us to give Mr. Sato the map, or get his help somehow, but that wasn't it at all. He was telling us to beware of this man. Mr. Sato, he wants the land!"

"What land is he talking about?"

"Dr. Makaha had narrowed his search for the king to a couple areas. Apparently, one is in a very beautiful part of the island and developers want to build a hotel there."

129

A very worried look came over Alana's mom's face.

"Where are Alana and Wyatt?" she asked. "Please tell me they are here at the park with you?"

"No, they went to Volcanoes National Park. Kalani told us one of the symbols on the map had to do with Kīlauea so they went to investigate."

"Why didn't Alana call me?" she asked.

"The satellite phone wasn't working. It must have gotten damaged during our hike somehow. They told me to tell you they'd be back tomorrow night."

"We have to find them," she said, and went about gathering her things.

"Have you seen Mr. Sato lately?" I asked, slinging my backpack over my shoulders.

"Not since you left for the Waipi'o Valley."

"Oh, jeez. This is all starting to make sense. I bet he was the one trying to scare us last night."

"Scare you? What do you mean?"

"Before we left, he told us about this Hawaiian curse and I'm pretty sure he was snooping around our tent last night. Probably hoping we'd be so scared that we'd hand over the map. And if it was him, I bet he followed Wyatt and Alana to the park!"

"Come on, we have to go. My jeep is out back."

It's about an hour and a half drive to Volcanoes National Park. We're making our way there now, and time seems to be standing still. I can't help but think Mr. Sato was somehow involved in Dr. Makaha's "accident" and if he gets to Wyatt and Alana before we do, their lives could be in danger!

WYATT

FEBRUARY 6, 10:19 PM
VOLCANOES NP
68° FAHRENHEIT, 20° CELSIUS

Dried lava bed in Volcanoes NP

The difference between a good explorer and a great explorer is the way one sees things. It doesn't matter if you are exploring the volcanic landscape of Hawaii or your own backyard, what's important is how well you notice the small details that most people overlook. It takes practice, but once you learn to see things on a deeper level it will significantly enhance all future adventures.

This is one of the things I learned from my dad. As a painter, he has trained himself to notice every detail of a scene. Maybe I also learned it by reading the journals of great explorers who kept such meticulous field notes. Whatever the case, while exploring it has always been my goal to take full account of my surroundings and document all findings.

I mention this now for a reason. Had I not taken the time to develop this skill, I might have never noticed the clues that led to our amazing discovery!

This afternoon we parked Alana's jeep and hiked deep into the park, exploring by flashlight the damp, meandering tunnel of the Thurston Lava Tube, then back into the bright sunlight, pushing our way through lush jungle, before hiking down a steep, dusty trail into a wide stretch of scorched landscape.

Walking atop an endless field of razor-sharp lava rocks slowed our pace. One wrong step will roll your ankle, or worse, snap it in two, so we were extra cautious.

Crossing this barren lava field, my legs took a beating, leaving me with several scrapes and bruises. Alana suffered some cuts, as well, but she is tough and did not complain once. About halfway to the ocean, the wind started to blow with great force. I've been in strong gales before, and though

I had no device to measure the wind speed, I would guess we faced gusts as high as forty miles per hour today.

The landscape seemed almost void of life, and yet this is one of the places where the earth is most alive. Lava flows just below the dark layer of the earth's crust. Among the jagged black rocks, sprouts of new green grass and even trees force their way up through the cracks—all a promising reminder of nature's resilience.

After nearly two hours, we arrived at the end of the dried lava flow. Just ahead, over a mound of rocks, thick clouds of steam rose into the sky.

"This is the place where Kīlauea meets the sea," Alana said. "Kalani pointed it out on the map. Just over those rocks, we'll be able to see the lava, so be careful. One misstep and we're burnt toast."

She wasn't kidding.

The heat was intense as we scrambled to the top of the rocks and looked over the edge. A couple hundred feet below, in a narrow canyon, was a meandering river of glowing lava. My jaw dropped at the sight. The river was like an uncoiled snake, lit orange-red with streaks of black that morphed and changed shape. At the tongue of the river, molten rock spilled slowly over a low cliff like neon molasses. Where water met fire, the ocean fizzed, sputtered, and popped. Steam floated upward and was carried away by the wind.

All around the steam, a luminous blue-green sea heaved and lurched, the occasional wave crashing against the rocks and sending spray inland. High cliffs dropped into the water behind us, and further down was an almost hidden cove, with calm waters and a pristine sandy beach that ran in the shape of a half-moon. Framing the beach was a forest of high palms, bent inland by the Pacific winds.

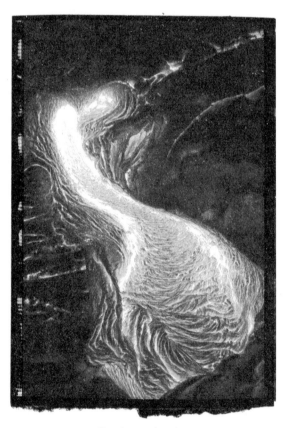

Flowing molten lava

"How hot is that lava?" I asked Alana.

"Between 1,300 and 2,200 degrees Fahrenheit. Come with me. We must make an offering to Pele the Fire Goddess."

Alana said a short prayer in Hawaiian, honoring Pele, the deity Hawaiians believe created the islands, then encouraged me to do the same.

"What should I say?" I asked.

"Take a moment to think about why you are here, to think about your purpose. Then Pele will know that you intend to do no harm."

Though I am skeptical of such ceremonies, I have a deep respect for the Hawaiian culture and went through with the procedure just as Alana had, thinking to myself as I did that this was just the sort of thing my brother would absolutely love.

When I was done with my offering, I'll admit, I felt good. It was exhilarating to be in this special place, the living land of the volcanoes. For ages lava has forced its way through the earth's crust, bubbling up from the ocean's depths—Pele's vent, as it's known—growing this spectacular island from miles underwater to almost fourteen thousand feet above the sea.

Stepping back from the heat, we sat down on a pair of uncomfortably jagged rocks.

"Can I take a look at the map?" Alana asked.

Reaching into my backpack, I retrieved the map and

handed it to Alana. While she looked it over, I grabbed my journal and reread all the notes I had written.

"What do you think Kalani meant by the wave's crest and a gem?" I asked.

We both looked out over the ocean, thinking. The sun had just dropped below the horizon. High waves rolled toward the shore. Steam rose into the darkening sky.

Sitting there, it dawned on me that the clues used to mark the location of the king's burial site may no longer even exist. An earthquake could have demolished them or they could have been covered by a more recent lava flow. I didn't want to consider this, not after all the work we'd done, and forced the thought from my mind.

"I don't know what to make of the clues," Alana said.

"I don't either. There are waves everywhere. And what are the chances we'd find a gem among all of this rock?"

"Not very good," Alana said, with a smile. "See that cliff to the south of us that drops off into the cove?"

I nodded.

"It was formed by a much older lava flow, and Kalani did mention the center of the cove. Let's see if we can climb down and walk along the beach. We'll camp down there tonight and continue our search in the morning. I bet there are some caves in the cliffs that we can explore. Maybe we'll find some more clues."

The climb down to the beach was treacherous. Approximately 250 feet high, the cliff had a steep pitch. The holds were sharp and some of the rocks were loose enough to pull free if you weren't careful. Descending a cliff wall is always more difficult than climbing up it. Fact is, that's when most climbing accidents happen. As I inched lower, my legs trembled and I became winded. The cut on my hand throbbed and my arm muscles burned. Before each step, Alana and I took the time to think through our next move and then checked to make sure the rock was stable before trusting it with our full weight. When we were about ten feet above the sand, I jumped and fell onto my back, completely exhausted. Alana fell down next to me and laughed. Both of us were relieved to be on safe ground.

The sky went dark as we rested. The moon is in its third quarter phase, and it cast a silvery reflection on the palms as they wiggled in the breeze. The cove ran in an almost complete circle, like a horseshoe, with the upper part open to the Pacific Ocean. High lava cliffs fortified the beach at the north and south ends. This place was paradise, even in the dark.

"Let's make our way to the middle of this beach and see if we find anything," Alana suggested. "Maybe that's the central point Kalani talked about."

"Sounds like a plan to me," I said.

By this time we were extremely thirsty. Wanting to preserve what was left of the water we'd brought with us, we walked into the palms, found two coconuts that had fallen and carried them back to the beach. Using my pocketknife,

I forced the blade inside the middle of the shell, creating a crack that ran a few inches on either side. Holding both ends of the coconut, I brought it down hard atop the sharp point of a lava rock. After several tries, the shell split. Quickly, I lifted the coconut over my mouth and pulled it apart at the crack to release the water. Alana did the same with her coconut. It was delicious and we both savored every drop.

Before pitching the shells, we used our pocketknives to scrape away chunks of the coconut's interior white lining. Slightly sweet and slimy, coconut "meat," as it's called, contains essential nutrients and makes for a good snack. It was just what we needed after our grueling trek.

I'd almost polished it off, when I looked up to the sky. There they were, right before my eyes—the stars that were on the map!

"Look, Alana," I said and pointed at the sky. "The Big Dipper."

"And the North Star," she said. "Do you think they might help us find the burial site?"

"Let's take a look at the map."

I took out the map, unfolded it and turned on my headlamp.

"Look how it's drawn," I said, tracing the stars. "See the Big Dipper's position? If this circle was a clock and you drew a line from the North Star directly over the two pointer stars, the line would point at the seven, right?"

"Yes, I see that."

"That could mean something."

For a moment, we both stood quietly thinking about the clues. I looked around the cove, to the right and then to the left. We were standing in the very center of the cove's beach, the same location that was marked on the map. That's when it occurred to me.

"I need to find a stick," I said. "Or anything with a straight edge."

We both searched around in the dark.

"Here," Alana said, tearing a frond from a palm bush. "Use this."

"Perfect."

I held the palm frond to the sky. Putting the higher end at the North Star, I brought the lower end of the frond down at exactly seven o'clock.

"Look, if you were to line up the stars like they're drawn on the map, they point directly into those cliffs on the other side of the cove."

"That could be why the center of this beach is marked on the map," Alana said. "Because seven o'clock will fall in different locations depending on where you're standing."

"Makes sense."

"Let's go check it out."

Navigating the rocks along the shore, we made our way to the cliff.

"Okay," I said. "This is the place."

I took a flashlight out of my backpack and shined it along

the cliff wall. After a few minutes, I noticed a distinct geological formation about fifteen or so yards from where we stood.

"Alana, look," I said, and shined the flashlight's beam along the wall.

Tucked under the cliff was a very unique stretch of black rock, curled over in the shape of a wave.

"Do you see what I see?" I asked.

"It looks like a wave of lava," she said.

"Do you think that's the symbol on the map?" I asked.

"Only one way to find out."

We both took off, scrambling over the rocks. As we approached the lava formation, an entirely different sort of wave swept over me; a wave of unease. Could we actually be closing in on the final resting place of King Kamehameha the Great? It was hard to imagine.

The lava curled overhead and ran further back under the cliff, like a tube, growing narrower the deeper it went. We set our backpacks down and Alana took the lead, crouching down as she moved inside. About halfway through it, we had to squat down on our hands and knees in order to go any further. The rocks above and below were mangled and jagged, with some edges as sharp as razors. The bandaged cut on my hand started to throb, so I pulled my shirtsleeve down over the top to try to keep from reopening the wound.

"I can't go any further," Alana said. "It's too narrow."

"Have you seen anything to make you think this is a sacred burial site?" I asked.

"No, I haven't. Have you?"

"No."

"Let's turn back. Maybe we missed something."

Carefully, I inched backwards, trying to avoid scraping my back against the rocks overhead. Once there was more space, I turned around and crawled forward. When I looked up my headlamp beam met a stone, sending a bright burst of light across the tunnel.

"Alana, did you see that?"

"No," she said. "What was it?"

Slowly, I turned my head, moving the lamplight back across the top of the cave. Again, it hit something in the rocks that shot a beam of light through the tunnel. Focusing my lamp on this area, I finally saw what appeared to be a smooth black stone at the highest point in the wave.

"A gem at the crest of the wave," I said almost to myself.

"What?" Alana asked.

"The wave, the wave's crest, and a gem!" I said. "Look up there!" Again I directed my headlamp at the stone and pointed. "Doesn't that look like a gemstone?"

"It does."

Alana and I moved underneath the stone. At closer inspection, the stone looked like a piece of black glass or polished lava.

"All the clues lead to this place," I said, my hands now trembling. "This has to be it, Alana!"

Alana combed the cave with her headlamp.

"But I don't see anything else," she said. "Do you?"

"No, I don't."

"I guess it's possible the king's remains could have washed away in a tidal surge."

"That's true, but would he have been laid to rest out in the open?"

"No, he would have been hidden away, most likely. According to ancient tradition, there would have been a ceremony to prepare his body for burial. This included removing the flesh from the bones, then wrapping the bones for burial."

"Maybe there's another cave or chamber in here somewhere."

We continued to search. It appeared the lava wave had only one way in and one way out. There were no other visible tunnels extending from it. I began to think Alana was right, that King Kamehameha's bones might have been washed away at some point over the past two centuries.

I moved back under the smooth black stone to observe it more closely and saw that it came to a sharp point on one end. I pushed gently against the point with my finger, wondering about the significance of this gem as a clue. That's when I noticed that the sharp end pointed to a pile of black sand that had gathered against the back of the rocks.

"See the point on the black stone?" I asked.

"Yes," Alana said.

"What if that points to where the king's bones were placed?"

Alana looked over at the pile of sand.

"Should we remove the sand and see if there's anything behind it?" I asked.

"I think we should," Alana said.

Alana and I crawled over and carefully scooped away handfuls of sand, revealing what looked like a small area that had been chipped away and refilled with stones.

"I have a feeling we're really close," Alana said. "The king's bones and all his mana could be right inside this chamber!"

Again, I don't necessarily believe in the idea of mana or the transferring of spiritual power. That said, out of respect, I asked Alana what she thought we should do.

"I'll admit," she replied, "I'm a little nervous."

"I understand. Kalani said we could set off a 'storm of spiritual unrest' if the king's remains were disturbed, so I just want to make sure we do everything right."

Alana took a deep breath.

"I think it will be okay, as long as we don't move the king's bones," she said.

"Are you sure you're comfortable with this?" I asked.

"Yes, I'm sure."

One by one we lifted and set aside the stones that were wedged into the small chamber. The anticipation was building as the chamber opened up. I could sense the anxiety in Alana and noticed that I was holding my breath.

As we cleared away the rocks, the edge of what looked like a smooth stone box was revealed. With shaky hands, I removed the remaining rocks and gently swept away more sand. Before us, tucked snugly into the chamber, was a perfectly preserved rectangular stone chest, about the size of a traveler's suitcase. There was no inscription on it, but it had certainly been put there for a reason. Atop the chest was a stone slab that looked like it could easily be removed.

"Do we open it?" I asked Alana.

"We need to take a look inside," Alana said, "but we have to be very careful."

Alana and I both took a deep breath and grabbed hold of the stone slab.

"Okay, ready?" she asked.

"Ready."

Together, we slid the top off of the chest. Dust swirled in my headlamp. Outside the cave, waves thundered. As soon as we could see into the chest, we stopped sliding the stone. Alana gasped and pointed. She was too startled to speak.

There, inside the chest, was a bone.

A human bone!

Also inside was a piece of canvas-like material wrapped around what I imagined must be the rest of the remains. The bone that was visible stuck out of the wrapping at the bottom. It was white mostly, brittle seeming, with brown and gray streaks. As best I could tell without touching it, the bone was from the lower part of the leg, the femur.

"There's nothing here noting that this is King Kame-hameha," I said. "No carving or inscription. How can we be absolutely sure this is him?"

"Kalani had heard of a map that marked the king's burial site," Alana said. "And he believed this map could very well be the one. All the clues on the map point to this place. We have to assume this is it. I think we've done it, Wyatt. I think we've found King Kamehameha the Great!"

Alana bowed her head and said a prayer for the king in Hawaiian.

I bowed my head, as well, quietly paying my respects to one of Hawaii's greatest leaders.

"Let's put the top back just the way it was," Alana said. "I've promised the king his burial site will not be disturbed."

Carefully, we slid the top back in place and closed off the chamber, refilling it with the stones.

"My hands won't stop shaking," Alana said.

I was feeling shaky myself.

"We should probably get going," I said. "If you're up for it, I think we should hike back to your jeep instead of camping on the beach. The sooner we get word of this to your mom, the better. She can help make sure the appropriate steps are taken to protect the area."

"I wouldn't be able to sleep anyway," Alana said, looking at her watch. "It's 8:45 p.m. If we make good time, we could be back to the ranger station by midnight."

Due to the darkness, the climb back up the cliff and trek over the lava field has been more difficult that the trek in, but we have still made good time. Our legs are shot, so we sat to rest and refuel with some dried fruit and nuts we brought in our backpacks. Alana and I decided it was also critical to get this all down in my journal before we forgot a single detail, so I've been writing constantly since we stopped.

We're seated in a pocket of sand among the lava rocks, still probably 30-45 minutes from the jeep. My body is so fatigued I don't even want to get up, but we're both very anxious to get news to Alana's mom. We can't stop. We have to keep going . . .

GANNON

Volcanoes National Park, 12 miles.

That's what it said on the last road sign we passed. We're getting close and plan to drive every road in the park until we find Alana's jeep. Fingers crossed we find Alana and Wyatt, too. Fingers and toes crossed we find them safe.

WYATT

FEBRUARY 7, 12:28 AM
VOLCANOES NP,
72° FAHRENHEIT, 22° CELSIUS

After a lengthy rest, we continued through the lava field, stepping cautiously from rock to rock. When we finally made it back to Alana's jeep, our relief immediately turned to terror.

Her tires had been slashed!

At first Alana thought she might have run over something that punctured the tires. After a close examination, however, it's obvious that all four tires were intentionally lacerated with some kind of knife. The interior of the jeep was ransacked, as well. Strangely, nothing was taken.

It is late and would not be smart to try to hike all the way back to the ranger station in the dark. It's just too far, so we've hunkered down about fifty yards from the jeep and decided to stay put until first light.

Considering the strange rock pyramids that were erected outside our tent in the Waipiʻo Valley and now Alana's jeep tires being flattened, it's pretty clear that we are being followed. Tonight, we've taken extra precautions to make sure we are not found, each of us hiding in a narrow stretch of black sand. My hiding spot is about fifteen feet from Alana's and both of us are surrounded on all sides by large rocks. Lying among these rocks, it seems almost impossible that we would be found unless someone happened to hike right over the top of us, and that doesn't seem likely in the dark.

I am trying to keep my composure, but it's been a challenge. Fact is, we don't feel safe. Someone is after us, and we're scared. If there's one positive, a silver lining so to speak, it's that Gannon isn't with us. If he were, we'd be dealing with some serious drama right now.

At sunrise we will begin our trek out. From here, Alana says we're about twenty miles from the ranger station. A strenuous hike, even in the daytime. Somewhere along the way, though, we expect to run into a park ranger or kind traveler who might give us a lift.

As for now, it's time to get some rest. As tired as I am, I can hardly wait for the sun to rise so we can get out of here.

GANNON

VOLCANO HOUSE
AFTER MIDNIGHT

A more recent lava flow

We cruised every road Mrs. Aukai knew within Volcanoes National Park, shining a powerful spotlight as we drove. Still, we found nothing. No sign of Alana's jeep anywhere, which makes us think they've gone off trail somewhere.

Alana's mom called the park ranger station and asked around, but didn't have any luck until we stopped at the Volcano House. When she described her daughter, the woman at the front desk said Alana had been at the hotel earlier and called the ranger that she had seen talking to her. He was in the barracks and had already gone to bed for the night, since it was almost midnight by this time, but the woman at the front desk could sense Mrs. Aukai's concern, so she asked that the ranger be woken. Turns out this ranger knew Alana's family. His name was Alapaki and when he heard Mrs. Aukai was looking for her daughter, he came right over.

"Aloha," Alapaki said as he approached, still looking a little groggy.

"Aloha," Alana's mom said. "Thank you so much for coming. I am really sorry to disturb your sleep."

"It's no trouble," he said. "So, you haven't heard from Alana since she arrived at the park?"

"No, we haven't. Did she tell you where she was going?"

"She didn't. I saw her in the lobby earlier and stopped to say hello. She seemed in a bit of a hurry, so we didn't talk for long. Why, are you concerned?"

"She and a young explorer named Wyatt are on an archeological expedition and I'm afraid they might be in danger."

"I've known Alana for a long time," Alapaki said. "She is cautious, smart and knows the island as well as anyone. I am sure she and Wyatt are just fine."

"It's just . . ." Mrs. Aukai trailed off.

"What is it?"

"We think someone might be after them," Mrs. Aukai finally said.

"For what reason?" Alapaki asked.

"It's a complicated story," Mrs. Aukai said. "I'll explain when the time is right, I promise. But first we need to find them. What time did you see Alana?"

"It was during my break, so probably around two-thirty this afternoon," he said. "I bet she signed today's log book before entering the park. She knows the dangers of back-country travel and would never leave on an expedition without making note of where she was going."

"Good thinking," Mrs. Aukai said. "Where is the log book?"

"It's filed away in the office. Let's go have a look."

In the office, Alapaki took the log book off the shelf. Opening it to today's date, we browsed through a short list of names written on the page. Sure enough, at 2:47 p.m. Alana and Wyatt had registered their names. Alana's note read, "We plan to explore Kīlauea, hike to where the lava meets the sea, camp overnight, and return by tomorrow afternoon, February 8."

"I can take you to this place," Alapaki said. "But it involves a long hike, so we will have to wait until daylight. At sunup, we can retrace their steps until we find them."

"Okay," Mrs. Aukai said. "That will have to do."

"Does everyone who enters the park have to sign the log book?" I asked.

"Yes, we strongly encourage all hikers and campers to sign the book," Alapaki said.

Mrs. Aukai and I scanned all the names on the list. My heart was thumping in my chest, as I expected to see the name "Sato" somewhere below Alana and Wyatt's, but it wasn't anywhere on the page.

"Why do you ask?" Alapaki said.

"I was just curious," I replied, looking up from the book. I think Alana's mom and I were both slightly relieved. Maybe he wasn't following them after all. But then a thought occurred to me. If Mr. Sato had actually followed Alana and Wyatt into the park with the intention of stealing the map from them, he would have never signed his actual name.

"Please go get some sleep," Mrs. Aukai said to Alapaki. "Again, I apologize for waking you."

"Let's meet here in the lobby at 5:30 a.m." Alapaki said. "Elaina at the front desk will show you to the ranger guest quarters." Alapaki placed his hand on Alana's mom's shoulder. "Alana and Wyatt will be okay. I have faith."

"Thank you," she said. "Aloha ahiahi."

"Aloha ahiahi."

WYATT

I awoke in the dark to see a shiny spear, only inches from my face. The flat side of the metallic spear flickered in the moonlight as it was drawn back and thrust at my throat. I gasped and closed my eyes, thinking my life was over!

When I opened my eyes again, the spear remained, held steady and at close range. My entire body seized with fear. Holding the spear was a shirtless man wearing the mask of an ancient Hawaiian warrior. It was made of wood, with circular eyes, black stripes across the cheeks, and strands of beads dangling over the mouth and chin. Attached to the top of the mask and sticking straight up were fiery red feathers.

Gannon's story of the night marchers immediately came to mind. Even though I had dismissed it as a myth I could not, in this sleep-deprived state of panic, rule out completely that this might, in fact, be the spirit of an ancient warrior.

"Where's the girl?" the figure whispered.

"She hiked out to find help," I said, hoping to protect Alana.

"Then you come with me."

I stood up as ordered and moved with this masked figure into the dark volcanic landscape. Glancing over, I caught sight of Alana in the distance, sleeping soundly between the rocks. As desperate as I was to yell out Alana's name and tell her to run for help, doing so would give up her location and put her in grave danger. Instead, I turned in the opposite direction and moved us further away from where she slept.

A band of color stretched across the low horizon. It was early morning and would be light soon, but the visibility was minimal and in my haste I'd left my headlamp in the sand. I was forced to walk ahead and nearly tripped over a rock in the darkness.

"I can't see very well," I said. "It's hard to keep my footing."

"Just keep moving," the figure said in a haunting voice, and nudged me gently in the back with the point of the spear. Feeling the sharp tip, I jumped forward, not wanting it to puncture my skin.

After a brief march, I was pushed up a slope of rocks to an open vent. Below me was a small hole that fell deep into the earth. A pool of lava at the base bubbled and spit geysers of molten rock into the air.

With the spear, I was nudged out to the edge of the rocks. Scorching heat rose up from the lava. I broke into a sweat. The steam brought a weakness to my knees. One more nudge with the spear and I would fall to my death.

"Please, don't!" I shouted, my voice shaky.

"You have something of mine," said a scratchy voice.

"What do I have?"

"The map!"

I paused for a second, and tried to think of the best way

to respond. Choose the right words and my life might be spared. Choose the wrong words and it would be all over.

"Hand it over now!" he shouted, obviously growing impatient.

"I don't have it," I said.

I was nervous and just trying to buy time. Fact is, I was lying. The map was in the pocket of my pants.

"Then I'll send you to Pele and go find the girl," he said, and came at me with the spear. I dodged it and nearly lost my footing. I felt I had no choice but to give him what he wanted.

"Wait, stop!" I yelled. "I'll give you the map!"

I needed to give myself a fighting chance. The best way, I thought, was to flip the situation in my favor. I took the map out of my pocket and held it high over my head.

"If I go in, the map comes with me!" I shouted.

"No more games," he said, in an angry tone. "Give it to me now."

"Promise me that you'll let me go, and I'll give it to you!"

"I'm not making any promises!"

"You have to if you want the map!"

His forearm muscles rippled as he tightened his grip on the spear. I dangled the map over the lava.

"I'll have you know that the map you're holding is price-less," he said. "It tells the location of King Kamehameha's sacred burial site."

"But why would you be willing to kill me for it?"

"The king's land is worth far more to me than your life, that's why!"

He thrust his spear just to the right of my shoulder. It seemed he was trying to move me away from the cliff's edge so that he could finish me off and take the map. I held my position the best I could, but my footing was unstable. Each time he lunged at me with the spear I was at risk of falling over.

"Please, put the spear down! I'll give you the map, but it's no good to you if I'm dead! I'm the only one who can make sense of the clues! Without that information, this map is useless to you!"

"Hand it over now! Your fate depends on how well you cooperate!"

Again, I lifted the map, letting it flutter over the cliff.

"And what if I don't cooperate at all?" I asked.

The masked warrior became so irate he let out a primal scream. I stuffed the map back into my pocket just as he charged me with his spear. In an instant, I moved aside, dodging the blade by mere inches. As the spear went past, I grabbed it with both hands. The masked warrior and I were face-to-face, struggling over control of the spear, while teetering on the edge of the cliff. One misstep and we would both fall into the lava. I strained with all my might to keep from being overpowered. The man was strong, but given all that was at stake, I experienced a bout of adrenaline-induced super-strength, and was able to hold my own.

Then, unexpectedly, he smashed me in the face with his wooden mask. A direct head-butt to the nose! My eyes watered and my legs went wobbly. I dropped to my knees, still holding on to the spear. The man now had the upper hand. I was losing the battle.

The head-butt had been so hard it loosened the mask, which suddenly swung away from his face and dangled around his neck.

The masked warrior . . . it was Mr. Sato!

Because I would be able to identify him to the police, I knew he had no intention of letting me go. He basically had one option, and that was to send me to a fiery grave!

As hard as I struggled, I was being overpowered. Mr. Sato pushed me closer to the edge. Rage filled his eyes.

As I fought for my life, I thought I heard a voice.

I did.

Someone was shouting!

"Wyatt!" I heard. "We're coming!"

I'd know that shrill voice anywhere. It was Gannon!

Looking over, I saw my brother, Alana, Mrs. Aukai and a park ranger. They were scrambling over the rocks, making their way to us.

Mr. Sato pressed the shaft of the spear against my throat. I couldn't breathe.

"I'll get that map one way or another," he said through clinched teeth.

"Don't do it," I blurted, choking. "Please!"

Possessed by anger, Mr. Sato would not let up. In fact, he pressed even harder. I was seconds away from losing consciousness.

"Stop!" Gannon screamed.

Startled, Mr. Sato turned to him. Gannon had a lava rock the size of a soccer ball held over his head, ready to bring it down on Mr. Sato if need be. The park ranger stood directly behind Gannon.

"If you hurt my brother, you're going into the lava!" Gannon yelled.

In a flash, Mr. Sato jumped up to face Gannon, pulling the spear away from my neck. I gasped for air. Mr. Sato brought his arm back, and was about to throw the spear at my brother.

"No!" the park ranger screamed.

Stepping back, Mr. Sato's heel caught on a rock and he lost his balance. The spear fell from his hand and landed on the ground. I could see the terror in Mr. Sato's eyes as he stumbled. His momentum was taking him backwards. He was going to fall into the pool of lava!

I had a choice to make and only a split second to make it. I could try to prevent his fall or allow him to plummet to his death.

Mr. Sato reached out for me, his eyes pleading for help. Knowing what I had to do, I sprang forward and threw my arm toward his. Fortunately, I was able to grab hold of his wrist and pull him away from the edge. He fell to the ground, panting.

The park ranger picked up the spear and pointed it at Mr. Sato. So shaken by what had just occurred, I couldn't keep from voicing my anger.

"How does it feel to be on the other end of the spear?" I shouted.

Mr. Sato said nothing.

Gannon, Alana and Mrs. Aukai were all armed with lava rocks and ready to pelt Mr. Sato if he tried to get away.

"We've got you surrounded," the park ranger said. "Additional rangers have been notified of our location and should be here shortly. Stay where you are and you won't get hurt."

"Dr. Makaha warned us that you were dangerous!" Gannon said.

"Dr. Makaha?" Mr. Sato said, his voice trembling. "Is he . . . is he still alive?"

"It looks like he's going to pull through."

"I didn't mean for him to fall into the ocean!" Mr. Sato confessed. "I just wanted the map and he refused to turn it over to me. A scuffle started over it and he went off the cliff! I swear it was an accident!"

"Tell it to the authorities," Mrs. Aukai said. "When Dr. Makaha is better, we'll get his side of the story, too."

Mr. Sato's head sank. He would soon be facing several criminal charges, including, possibly, two counts of attempted murder.

I looked over at Mrs. Aukai and Gannon. Now that I was out of danger, a smile spread across my face.

"Wait until you see what Alana and I found," I said.

"Alana told me," Mrs. Aukai said, with a grin. "Truly amazing! You all have done the Hawaiian Islands and its people a great service!"

GANNON

FEBRUARY 8, LATE NIGHT
VOLCANOES NATIONAL PARK
VOLCANO HOUSE, ROOM #6

Okay, to say this has been a whirlwind of an adventure would be a huge understatement. It's been so much more than that. I mean, parts of the trip were relaxing and therapeutic and others were so totally insane and preposterous that we're lucky to have made it out alive.

Seriously, it's hard to even comprehend, so at this stage I think I need to take a little time to get the latest developments down in my journal, just to try to make sense of it all.

Right, so, when Alapaki, Mrs. Aukai, and I found Alana's jeep with her tires slashed, oh man, we just about flipped out, but fortunately Alana heard all our commotion and came running from where she had hidden for the night. She was freaking out herself and told us that my brother was missing!

Well, that led to a mad scramble over lava rocks, which then led to the discovery of Mr. Sato struggling with Wyatt over a big, bubbly, belching pool of lava! Luckily, we arrived just in time to prevent either of them from being incinerated, and thank goodness for that. I mean, as much as Wyatt can get on my nerves, the last thing I want is to see him go up in flames like a matchstick!

I'm happy to report that Mr. Sato is now under arrest and in jail, which is exactly where he deserves to be. It was just like Mrs. Makaha said, a group of greedy hotel developers wanted the land. They had plans to build a megaresort, and were willing to do whatever it took to make it happen. So, when Dr. Makaha was able to postpone the hotel from being built so that he could continue his search, Mr. Sato was hired to quickly find and hide the bones of King Kamehameha. With no evidence of a sacred burial site, the government would ultimately agree to open the land for development. For his work, Mr. Sato was being paid several million dollars. Goes without saying, but doing business this way is totally illegal and will probably add several more years to what I'm guessing will be a long prison sentence for Mr. Sato.

After the park rangers arrived on the scene, Wyatt and Alana took us back to the burial site. It's tucked into a tubular-shaped lava cave near one of the most beautiful beaches in the world. It seemed like the perfect place for a king to be laid to rest, but just to make sure, scientists have been called in to conduct a test that will determine once and for all if the remains are actually those of King Kamehameha the Great. And with the advanced equipment they have today, the scientists can run this test without disturbing the remains, which makes everyone happy. If it proves to be the King, we were told the government will quickly pass a law to preserve the burial site and surrounding land forever.

That's right, FOREVER!

Oh, and one last bit of totally awesome news. Dr. Makaha's condition continues to improve. He's regained his speech, is able to walk slowly, and should be able to go home real soon! From what Mrs. Makaha told me, he explained to police that he never trusted Mr. Sato, and told them how he had been thrown into the ocean when the two men were struggling over possession of the map. Turns out, Dr. Makaha had discovered the map years ago while searching through archives in a basement on the University of Hawaii campus. He had mostly kept the map a secret. He wanted to study it himself, and not alert anyone who might wish to use it for their own personal gain, like Mr. Sato, who only learned of the map's existence after breaking into Dr. Makaha's office and reading his field notes.

Oh, and get this. Turns out Mr. Sato is a total scam artist. He doesn't have a master's degree in anthropology and he doesn't work for the Smithsonian either. The guy forged all his credentials so that he could join Dr. Makaha's expedition and convince everyone that the king's remains were not anywhere near that beautiful beach. I mean, what kind of a person does something like that?

The map will again be archived in the University's vault

until they decide whether or not to put it on display for the public. We're going to visit Dr. Makaha in Honolulu while we're there for the language workshop at the Cultural Center. I can't wait to talk to him and his family again. Given the way we met, I have a feeling we'll be friends for a long time.

All righty, then. Time to get some zzz's. Just knowing that we're safe from night marchers and ancient Hawaiian curses and the corrupt and potentially murderous men who were after the map, I think I might finally get a decent night's sleep!

Catch you later . . .

WYATT

FEBRUARY 9, 1:14 PM

We just received official word.

Without disturbing the burial site, the scientists were able to verify that the bones do, in fact, belong to King Kamehameha the Great! Alana and I were fairly confident, so I can't say I didn't expect this news, but I'm still in a mild state of shock.

According to the *Honolulu Star*, a law is already being drafted by the Hawaiian Congress that will protect the land from future development. This law is expected to pass without debate. The article also reported that Mr. Sato and several of the hotel developers are being held in the Hilo jail without bond. Their trial has been set for early May.

"Thanks to your investigative work, bravery, and consideration for the beliefs and wishes of the Hawaiian people, this incredible discovery was handled better than anyone could have hoped," Mrs. Aukai said. "You should be proud knowing that a hotel will never be built on that gorgeous and sacred Hawaiian beach. King Kamehameha would be very grateful for all you have done."

Waves crashing along the shore

GANNON

HAPUNA BEACH

Aloha!

Oh, man. I just love saying that, or writing it, or whatever. In my opinion, it's one of the greatest words ever invented.

I woke early this morning with the Aloha Spirit pulsing through my veins, and since it's our last day on the Big Island, it seemed only right that we do something that was one hundred percent authentically "Hawaiian."

Well, since Hawaiians were reported to be the first true "wave riders," Wyatt and I decided to spend the morning surfing. Then again, I'm not sure I'd call what we did *surfing*. It might be more accurate to call it "falling" or "wiping out" or "getting pummeled by the waves." Sure, we caught a few of the smaller waves and managed okay on them, but after getting sloshed around like a pair of shorts in a washing machine, I decided it's probably best if my brother and I stick to exploration and leave the wave riding to those who know what the heck they're doing.

For me, the best part of surfing might have been the quiet time spent sitting atop our boards, 150 feet or so offshore, waiting for another set of waves to roll in. To see the island from the water gives you a whole new perspective on the place. The sandy beach, tall palms, and rolling hills all split by dried gray-black rivers of lava that snake their way to the sea. And further up, almost unimaginably, a mountain peak capped with snow. I've said it before and I'll say it again, *this place is paradise!*

Taking in all that beauty got me thinking about Hawaii's future. In a place that attracts so many tourists, can a balance be struck between growth and development and the preservation of nature and culture? Maybe it's like Alana said, "We cannot stop progress. It is inevitable. So instead of fighting progress, we must embrace it, while being mindful of nature and allowing Hawaiian values to guide the changes that occur."

Mālama 'āina is another phrase I love. It means "to care for the land." Being good stewards of the environment is obviously a very important concept in Hawaiian life, and probably the key to a healthy and prosperous future, not just here on the islands, but all over the world.

Well, we've just about come to the end of our stay on the Big Island, but before we go we're joining the Aukai family at a traditional Hawaiian luau. It's been impossible to reach my dad since he's living off the grid and all, but a friend of Mrs. Aukai was apparently able to get word to him about tonight's celebration. Oh, man, I can't wait to see him and tell him all about our adventure. Pretty sure he's going to flip! Tomorrow we leave to meet my mom in Honolulu for a course in Hawaiian language and culture. When she hears about everything that's happened since she left, I'm sure she's going to flip, too!

A sea turtle resting on the beach

As for my thoughts on what I've learned so far, I have to believe that if people continue to support cultural and environmental preservation here on the islands, important things like the Hawaiian language and the Aloha Spirit and all the endangered bird species will not just survive for generations to come, they will thrive.

WYATT

FEBRUARY 10, 10:33 PM

Nothing humbles a rhythmically challenged person more than being asked to dance. The fact that it was in front of a couple hundred people only made it more embarrassing. The hula is a serene and graceful Hawaiian dance. At least, it is when it's done by people who can actually dance. When I do it, not so much.

The movements of hula are slow and fluid. They symbolize the wind, waves, and spirits, as well as the coming together of all the Hawaiian Islands. As the author Paul Theroux wrote, "Hula is Aloha in action . . . it's history, it's society, it's mythology, and it's a way of being happy." And as Alana pointed out, hula dancing is another example of Hawaiians' deep connection with nature.

My dad made it to the luau just in time to see me being dragged up on stage. I tried my best to decline, but the dancers insisted. The next thing I know I'm wiggling my hips and waving my arms from side to side. They pulled Gannon up on stage, too, but lucky for my brother, he was born with enough rhythm to keep from humiliating himself when he dances. I, on the other hand, was born with zero rhythm and therefore, always humiliate myself when I dance.

Though they tried to hide their laughter, I could see Alana and her family chuckling behind their hands. It's okay, though, I would be laughing too if I were watching myself flounder around on stage.

The slow melody was soon replaced by an upbeat tempo, as several dancers began pounding away at their *pahu* drums. To keep pace with the rapid drumbeat, the speed of hula hip wiggling quickened. Honestly, it made me dizzy just to watch.

I was twirling and shaking, doing my best to keep up, when out of the corner of my eye I saw a circle of fire coming at me. As I jumped out of the way, a male dancer shuffled by spinning a fiery baton lit on both ends. I'd barely dodged the first fire dancer when I heard a voice behind me shout, "Comin' hot, bro!" I spun around just in time to narrowly avoid another wheel of flames, this one being spun by my brother.

I stepped back and watched, afraid Gannon would end up setting the whole stage on fire, but to tell the truth, he was actually pretty good with the baton. When he learned to do this, I don't have the slightest clue.

I guess it makes no difference. What's important is that my brother's performance took all the attention off my dancing, and allowed me to slip off stage. Alana and Mrs. Aukai both gave me a big hug for my effort. Alana's father, Eddie, and my dad laughed and smacked me on the back and we all watched in mild amazement as Gannon and another dancer burned orange circles in the air with their fiery batons.

The evening concluded with a brief, but moving ceremony where Gannon and I were symbolically adopted by Alana's family. We are now officially *hānai*, which means "adopted." This is a tremendous honor. I am truly humbled, and cannot thank our new Hawaiian friends enough for their kindness. As Gannon said, "Mahalo to all."

Walking back to our hotel room, my dad stopped Gannon and me.

"Look boys," he said, and pointed to the night sky.

"Oh my gosh, is that a rainbow?" Gannon asked.

"It's actually a moonbow," my dad explained. "Spectacular, isn't it?"

Arching high overhead and framed by stars, were all the colors of a daytime rainbow. Only difference is that this nighttime spectrum of color is caused by a refraction of moonlight, instead of sunlight. I had never seen such a thing in all my life and stood gazing in awed silence until, many minutes later, the moonbow faded from the sky.

When we first met Alana, she said that Hawaiians strive to embody the Aloha Spirit each and every day. That was inspiring to me. Given the positive power of the Aloha Spirit, its ability to spread happiness and make our everyday interactions with people and nature more meaningful, I think it is a goal that I must adopt myself.

So, in closing, I have one final thing to say:

Long live the "Aloha Spirit!"

ACKNOWLEDGMENTS

I would like to thank Dan and Mary Auki who welcomed me into their home in Kaneohe so many times. To Sui Lan, the matriarch of my Hawaiian 'ohana (and the woman who taught Don Ho to play the ukulele), and her husband John Fogarty, for his service at Pearl Harbor. Thank you to Leina, John, Margaret, and Peter Fogarty, my dearest Hawaiian 'ohana, who tried desperately to teach the hula to their haole hānai girl. Though you never quite succeeded, you blessed me with the beautiful meaning of *aloha*. Mahalo with all my heart! Keith would like to thank his great friend Neil Logan and his family for inviting him to their farm on the Big Island. The education they provided on the history and environment of the islands was invaluable. Lastly, we owe a debt of gratitude to Amy Kalili for providing us with a better understanding of the beautiful Hawaiian language. Mahalo to all!

GANNON & WYATT's

TRAVEL MAP

Siberia

St. Petersburg, Russia

Moscow, Russia

Gobi Desert, Mongolia

The Great Wall of China

Himalayas, Nepal

Masada, Israel

Tibet

Cairo, Egypt

Ruins of Petra, Jordan

Persian Gulf

Taj Mahal, India

Varanasi, India

Hong Kong, China

Angkor Wat, Cambodia

The Serengeti

Nairobi

Ngorongoro Crater

Kho Phi Phi, Thailand

Equator

Okavango Delta

Mauritius Islands

Bali

Darwin

Fiji

The Great Barrier Reef

Kalahari Desert

Australian Outback

Cape of Good Hope

Mt. Cook, New Zealand

Antarctica

McMurdo Station

THE HAWAIIAN LANGUAGE

If you would like to learn more about what is being done to preserve the Hawaiian language, or simply browse a wide offering of Hawaiian language resources, please visit ʻAha Pūnana Leo at **ahapunanaleo.org**.

Aloha!

Gannon and Wyatt in Hawaii

MEET THE "REAL-LIFE" GANNON AND WYATT

Have you ever imagined traveling the world over? Fifteen-year-old twin brothers Gannon and Wyatt have done just that. With a flight attendant for a mom and an international businessman for a dad, the spirit of adventure has been nurtured in them since they were very young. When they got older, the globetrotting brothers had an idea—why not share all of the amazing things they've learned during their travels with other kids? The result is the book series, Travels with Gannon & Wyatt, a video web series, blog, photographs from all over the world, and much more. Furthering their mission, the brothers also cofounded the Youth Exploration Society (Y.E.S.), an organization of young people who are passionate about making the world a better place. Each Travels with Gannon & Wyatt book is loosely based on real-life travels. Gannon and Wyatt have actually been to Greenland and run dog sleds on the ice sheet. They have kissed the Blarney Stone in Ireland, investigated Mayan temples in Mexico, and explored the active volcanoes of Hawaii. During these "research missions," the authors, along with Gannon and Wyatt, often sit around the campfire collaborating on an adventure tale that sets two young explorers on a quest for the kind of knowledge you can't get from a textbook. We hope you enjoy the novels that were inspired by these fireside chats. As Gannon and Wyatt like to say, "The world is our classroom, and we're bringing you along."

HAPPY TRAVELS!

Want to become a member of the

Youth Exploration Society

just like Gannon and Wyatt?

Check out our website. That's where you'll learn how to become a member of the Youth Exploration Society, an organization of young people, like yourself, who love to travel and are interested in world geography, cultures, and wildlife.

The website also includes:
Cool facts about every country on earth, a gallery of the world's flags, a world map where you can learn about different cultures and wildlife, spectacular photos from all corners of the globe, and information about Y.E.S. programs.

BE SURE TO CHECK IT OUT!
WWW.YOUTHEXPLORATIONSOCIETY.ORG

ABOUT THE AUTHORS

PATTI WHEELER, producer of the web series *Travels with Gannon & Wyatt: Off the Beaten Path,* began traveling at a young age and has nurtured the spirit of adventure in her family ever since. For years it has been her goal to create children's books that instill the spirit of adventure in young people. The Youth Exploration Society and Travels with Gannon & Wyatt are the realization of her dream.

KEITH HEMSTREET is a writer, producer, and cofounder of the Youth Exploration Society. He attended Florida State University and completed his graduate studies at Appalachian State University. He lives in Aspen, Colorado, with his wife and three daughters.

Make sure to check out the first five books in our award-winning series:

Botswana

Great Bear Rainforest

Egypt

Greenland

Ireland

Look for upcoming books and video from these and other exciting locations:

Australia

Cuba

Iceland

American Southwest

Don't forget to check out our website:

WWW.GANNONANDWYATT.COM

There you'll find complete episodes of our award-winning web series shot on location with Gannon & Wyatt.

You'll also find a gallery with spectacular photographs from Hawaii, Ireland, Greenland, Iceland, Egypt, the Great Bear Rainforest, and Botswana.

And wait, one more thing . . .

Check us out on Twitter, Pinterest, and

make sure to "like" us on Facebook!

With your parents' permission, of course.

PRAISE FOR
TRAVELS WITH GANNON & WYATT

"Each of us has the responsibility to protect and enrich our community, to ensure that future generations inherit a healthy and vibrant planet. In each action-packed book, *Travels with Gannon & Wyatt* communicates these values and inspires young people to do their part to help make the world a better place."

—Robert F. Kennedy Jr. (Series)

"Wheeler and Hemstreet pack this slim adventure full of facts and trivia, as well as photos and drawings, lending it an educational slant. With clear nods to *Indiana Jones* and other adventure stories, the fast-paced plot and engaging characters are sure to appeal to a young audience."

—Publishers Weekly (Egypt)

"*Travels with Gannon & Wyatt* is a phenomenal series that encourages the next generation of conservationists to push their boundaries and challenge themselves to explore life outside their comfort zones. A must read for any young person interested in the wild world of nature that sustains us all."

—Brigitte Griswold, director of youth programs,
The Nature Conservancy (Series)

"Twin teens explore various locations and introduce readers to the wonders, animals, and people of the places they visit. The books have a strong conservationist point of view, and the siblings encounter trouble not only from their natural surroundings but also from man-made threats to themselves and the environment. Each book also contains native people who help Gannon and Wyatt understand the areas they are exploring and, in some cases, help them survive. . . . The books focus primarily on painting a picture of the boys' travels and surroundings, and they do this well. The novels offer good entry points into these exciting worlds and should be enjoyed by anyone who likes reading about adventure and discovery."

—School Library Journal (Botswana, Great Bear Rainforest)

"Exceptionally well written and original, *Travels with Gannon & Wyatt: Greenland* is very highly recommended."

—Midwest Book Review (Greenland)

"This is the brilliant first of what I hope will be many in a travel-novel series. . . . Botswana has rarely had a portrayal that so accurately captures the physical and spiritual side of Africa."

—Sacramento Book Review (Botswana)

"This is a gripping novel featuring the land and culture of Greenland. . . . It packs a great deal of information into a short, suspenseful read that will appeal to fans of travel and adventure stories."

—School Library Journal (Greenland)

"Young, would-be adventurers or armchair travelers will enjoy exploring with these two straightforward, engaging personalities—and will learn a lot in the process."

—Kirkus Discoveries (Botswana)

"Written in the grand tradition of the Hardy Boys, Tom Swift, and Willard Price's adventure-seeking brothers Hal and Roger Hunt."

—Michelle Mallette, librarian and blogger,
Michelle's Bookshelf (Great Bear Rainforest)

"*Travels with Gannon & Wyatt* is a groundbreaking series of adventurous stories like nothing else ever seen in children's literature."

—Mark Zeiler, middle school language arts teacher, Orlando, Florida
(Series)

"It's the best book I've ever read!"

—Anna, 10 (Botswana)

"*Travels with Gannon & Wyatt: Botswana* is phenomenal! I read it in three hours!"

—Felix, 9 (Botswana)

"I loved the first three books, and I can't wait to read *Greenland*."

—Kipp, 9 (Egypt)

MY JOURNAL NOTES

Moloka'i

Lana'i

Maui

Kaho'olawe

Mauna Kea

Kailua-Kona ⊙

Hawai'i

Hilo ⊙

Volcanoes NP

Kaua'i

Ni'hau

O'ahu

Honolulu

HAWAII

PACIFIC
OCEAN

N